JACOB, KING OF PORTALIA

CASEY CLUBB

Booktrope Editions
Seattle, WA 2014

COPYRIGHT 2014 CASEY CLUBB

This work is licensed under a Creative Commons Attribution-Noncommercial-No Derivative Works 3.0 Unported License.

Attribution — You must attribute the work in the manner specified by the author or licensor (but not in any way that suggests that they endorse you or your use of the work).

Noncommercial — You may not use this work for commercial purposes.

No Derivative Works — You may not alter, transform, or build upon this work.

Inquiries about additional permissions should be directed to: info@booktrope.com

Cover Design by Greg Simanson

This is a work of fiction. Names, characters, places, brands, media, and incidents are either the product of the author's imagination or are used fictitiously. Any resemblance to similarly named places or to persons living or deceased is unintentional.

PRINT ISBN 978-1-62015-457-1

EPUB ISBN 978-1-62015-467-0

Library of Congress Control Number: 2014911359

DARE TO DREAM

SIXTH GRADE SUCKED.
 I was the smallest kid in school, as usual.
 Archer Middle School was twice the size of Beckman Elementary.
 And Sammy, my best and only friend, wasn't in any of my classes. For the first time ever.
 That meant that five days a week I had to make it through an entire day, all alone, with nowhere to hide.
 I didn't think my life could get any worse. But I was wrong about that. Very wrong.
 On the weekend of my twelfth birthday, I discovered just how very wrong I was.
 By the time I got home from school that Friday, it had already started. Earlier in the day, my best-kept secret had been discovered. Some of my worst fears were about to come true.
 I just didn't know it yet.
 I was enjoying an after-school peanut butter cup when Mom dropped the first bombshell.
 She did it as she was dabbing peroxide on the nasty scrape under my left armpit. I'd told her I'd tripped. From the way she pursed her lips, though, I could tell she wasn't fooled.
 "I talked to Mrs. Hendricks today," she said. I think she was hoping the sting of the antiseptic would distract me. It didn't.
 "Mrs. Hendricks runs the resource room," I said. I barely felt the peroxide.
 "She thinks you could benefit from support."
 "But resource room is before school."

"I know."

"Orchestra is before school." My fingers started twitching and I had to set my peanut butter cup down. "If I'm not in orchestra this year, I won't be able to get in next year, and...."

I hated going to school, knowing I wouldn't see Sammy for eight long hours. Orchestra was the only thing that got me to walk through the front doors every morning.

I'd been looking forward to orchestra ever since first grade.

All I've ever wanted to be is a musician. I figured if I worked hard enough and long enough it would happen.

After five years of private lessons and practicing every day, I was still waiting. Lately, it seemed like the more I tried, the worse I got.

But I wasn't worried. It was only because I hadn't grown into my ears yet.

Sammy said I was a very small boy in an extra big soul, like a baby mouse with big-mouse ears. I didn't fit into my soul yet. But I'd grow into it one day, just like I'd grow into my ears. And when I did, I'd play beautiful music, just like my father had.

My father had had big, pokey-out ears like me. He'd grown into them. And he'd made beautiful music. Someday, I would too.

I'd tried to explain about the ears to Mom, but she didn't understand.

"Honey, I know how much you want to be a musician, like your...." It was the closest she'd ever come to speaking of him. "But Fall Festival is next month."

That told me everything. Mr. Robertson, the orchestra director, didn't want me in Fall Festival. He kept asking if I was sure I wanted to play the violin. I told him I was. But he never seemed to like that answer.

"Mr. Robertson can't kick me out, not in sixth grade."

"*He's* not *kicking* you out. I'm *pulling* you out. You're behind in all your classes."

"But I'm still growing. And I've been practicing for over an hour every day."

"It's not that you haven't tried. And maybe if you put as much effort into your schoolwork as you do into your violin...."

We both knew that was a weak excuse. I sucked at school. Taking me out of orchestra wasn't going to improve my grades. It would only make my life more miserable.

"I know you have big dreams, Sweetie."

She said it like it was a bad thing. Sure, I had big dreams. And I knew that I had no talent to speak of. I had yet to find anything I didn't suck at, no matter how hard I tried. But that didn't mean I couldn't dream big.

I was going to be a musician. And not just an ordinary musician. I was going to be an intergalactic musician. I was going to travel to distant stars, visit other worlds and other people, and share beautiful music with them.

"You spend so much time hiding in that head of yours," Mom said. "Sometimes I wonder if you still know the difference between reality and fantasy."

Actually, I knew all about reality. That was why I had to hide.

I didn't want to have to hide. In fact, I wanted to live in a world where I could be *exactly* who I am and *not* have to hide any more. But I didn't live in that world. Hiding kept me safe. I'd been hiding all my life. How else did she think I'd survived this long?

Sammy was the best of all my hiding places. Without him, I had nowhere else to hide but in my head. Daydreaming kept me safe until I got home. To Sammy. And my clubhouse.

"Jacob, are you even listening?" Mom jiggled the table to get my attention. "See, this is what I'm talking about. Mrs. Hendricks says that you're always daydreaming. And when you're home, you spend all your time in that clubhouse of yours with Sammy. I'm not so sure that's a good thing."

I felt like she'd punched me in the gut. Harder, even, than Jimmy and his goons had this afternoon when they gave me an extra special pre-birthday knocking about.

Mom wasn't talking about orchestra anymore. She was talking about Sammy. And my clubhouse. Warning bells went off in my head.

"But it's my birthday weekend."

"I know."

"You promised that Sammy and I could spend the weekend in the clubhouse."

"I know I did." Amazingly, she looked like she'd hoped I'd forgotten.

"And you still can," she continued. "But I want you back in the house for Sunday dinner. And after that, we'll see."

Before I could say anything else, she started rearranging my hair with that faraway look that told me she was thinking of somebody else's head of unruly black hair, and someone else's mouse-like ears.

That was a bad sign, a very bad sign. I couldn't shake a sense of impending doom.

* * *

I crouched in an empty flowerbed at the back of the house. It was mucky, but beneath the master bedroom window was the only place I could listen in on my mom and step-dad without the twins catching me. At least it wasn't raining.

Rick sounded tired. "If he wears a shiny purple shirt to school, what does he expect?"

"That doesn't make it right," Mom said.

"I didn't say it did. But boys are like vultures. They can smell soft a mile away. And Jacob is way too soft. He has to grow a thicker skin."

"He's sweet and sensitive."

"He cries when a bird hits the window."

"Would you rather he laughed?"

"Baby, I'm not the enemy. But that boy is gutless. Sammy won't always be there to protect him. Jacob needs to learn to fend for himself, and soon, or he's going to get eaten alive. I'm worried about him. You know I love him like he's my own."

"I know you do."

I wasn't convinced. Rick had tried to bond with me through sports—another of my non-talents. But as soon as the twins were born, he shoved me aside like any other not-as-cool-as-you-thought-it'd-be toy. The twins were the cool toys that got loved forever and ever.

"I could throttle his father for what he's done to him," Rick said.

My heart lurched. I'd never heard Mom or Rick talk about my father. Not ever.

"He didn't have a choice," Mom said.

"All men have choices. He couldn't have picked a worse place to raise his son if he'd tried. And not just because of Jacob's year-round tan. He's getting more obvious."

"What do you mean?"

"You know what I mean." Rick sounded like it was far from the first time they'd had this conversation. "He never notices girls."

And that's when I knew it was all about to go horribly wrong.

"He's only eleven," Mom said.

"Twelve in three days. And he looks at boys the way boys are supposed to look at girls. At least, in this neck of the woods."

"You don't really think…?"

"I hope not, for his sake. Sammy's a great kid, but when he finds out, I'm not sure he'll stick around. People around here just aren't that kind of tolerant."

"I know."

"Are you still going to let them spend the weekend in the clubhouse?"

"I don't want to, but I already promised."

"He's getting older. He'll be thirteen next year."

There was a heavy silence, the kind you hear before someone receives a death sentence.

"I know," Mom said. "And after this weekend, I want you to board it up."

"You sure?"

"Yes. I can't do this anymore."

"Okay, I'll do it Monday." Rick sounded only too eager to agree.

I slipped to the ground. I thought I'd cried myself dry. I was wrong.

My father built the clubhouse for me just before he died. That and my orange-and-red rock were all I had of him. Now Mom wanted to take it from me.

But that wasn't why my body was shaking uncontrollably.

For years I've been terrified that someone would discover my secret.

It was my greatest fear. Because I knew that if Sammy found out, he wouldn't be my friend anymore. And Rick had just killed any hope I'd had that I was wrong about that.

If Rick had figured it out, Sammy would too.

I'd hidden it from everybody. I'd even tried to hide it from myself. Frantically, I tried to plan how I might hide harder and even better. But I didn't know that it was already too late.

Mom wasn't the only one intent on ruining my life. There was someone else too.

And earlier in the day, that person had stolen something from me and discovered my secret. By Monday, everyone would know. Even Sammy.

My life as I knew it was about to end.

MY FATHER'S GIFT

WHEN SAMMY GOT to the clubhouse, I grabbed my orange-and-red rock and joined him on the sofa. Sammy draped his arm over my shoulders and read his chemistry book.

My father had left me the strange rock. It used to be too big for me, like my ears were. But now, it fit just right in my palm, and I could almost wrap my fingers all the way around it.

I always needed something to keep my fingers occupied. Especially when I was nervous or scared. My father's orange-and-red rock had a texture that my fingers relished—a perfect balance between prickly and smooth as silk. It could keep my fingers happy for hours on end.

But what I love most about the rock is the way its musky cinnamon smell stirs up the most powerful and vivid memories of my father I've ever had.

My mother refuses to talk about my father. What little I know of him, I know from the memories that come to me. Most of them come to me in my sleep, in dreams that feel more like memories than dreams. But a few come to me when I'm holding my orange-and-red rock and savoring its smell. Those ones are the best.

Leaning back against Sammy, I held the rock close and took in a deep breath. As soon as its scent flooded me, I could see my father as clearly as if it were just yesterday. He was sitting on top of the clubhouse with me, tucking my hair behind my ears.

He looked just like me. He had the same tangled black hair and the same mouse ears. The only difference was that his no-sun-needed-tan was a few shades darker than mine.

We'd built the clubhouse together, he and I, built it with the big oak tree smack dab in the middle. We finished it just before my fourth birthday and we were going to celebrate by spending the weekend camping there, just the two of us.

But he drove off that day, and never came back.

I didn't get to spend that weekend in the clubhouse. But the next year, and every year since then, Sammy and I spent my birthday weekends camping in the clubhouse.

A lump formed in my throat. It was exactly eight years ago to the day that my father died. This would be the last year. My mother was going to take it all away.

Suddenly, the door slammed open and the Hurricane of Chaos swooped in. The loud burst of noise startled me and I dropped the rock with a surprised yelp.

The Hurricane of Chaos, otherwise known as David and Daniel, were my four-year-old manic twin half-brothers. Rick's precious sports prodigies.

They were all boy, not an ounce of softness in them. I doubted that Rick and Mom were worried they'd turn into gutless wonders. Or look at boys the wrong way.

Without breaking stride, the twins embarked on their mission of destruction. While David pounded on my piano, Daniel dumped a bag of chips on the floor and stomped them into dust. That kept him entertained for almost a full minute before he spied my rock.

Too late, I reached for it. Daniel beat me to it and scooped it up with a happy squeal.

"Give it back," I told him in my most commanding voice. One that sounded suspiciously mouse-like.

David merely giggled as if I'd said something funny.

Without even taking his eyes from his book, Sammy reached over and plucked the rock from Daniel's hand.

Before the twins could find bigger and better ways to destroy my clubhouse, Rick knocked at the door and ducked inside.

He surveyed the mess with an all-too-familiar look of disappointment. "Come on munchkins, time for bed." He sounded resigned. Like a man who was stuck with a spineless stepson he couldn't get rid of.

After they left, Sammy and I climbed up on the roof to gaze at the stars.

If I listened closely, I could hear the stars calling out to me, stirring my father's music within my soul. It was like he was talking directly to me, through the music of the stars, and I could almost believe he was sitting on top of the clubhouse with me and Sammy.

I'd always thought that if my dad had lived, we would have traveled to the stars together to play beautiful music.

That's why, for as long as I can remember, I've dreamt of being an intergalactic musician.

Mom called my dreams childish fantasies. But my dreams *weren't* fantasies. They were my link to my father. Without them, I feared I'd lose him forever.

I'd always known I would have to wait for my dreams to come true, and I'd been okay with that. Because I was still a small boy and I was still growing into my soul and my ears.

But who was I kidding? My ears weren't the only part of me that felt too big. No matter what it was or how hard I tried, nothing seemed to fit.

"Sammy, you don't think I'm crazy, do you?"

"Crazy? No." Sammy thumped me on the head. "Eccentric, absolutely. But I love you just the way you are, and you know it."

Sammy had never made me feel silly for my dreams. Although sometimes he gently pointed out that travel outside our solar system wasn't going to happen in my lifetime.

"You don't gotta go to the stars to be with your dad, Jakey. He built you this clubhouse to give you the stars right here. So you could share them with him always."

Sammy was right. That was the problem. Because Rick was going to board it up.

We didn't talk anymore after that. Somehow, even then, I think we both knew that it would be the last night we'd ever spend together in the clubhouse.

* * *

After wolfing down a large pizza, Sammy flopped back on the sofa. "Play for me, Jakey."

Sammy loved listening to me. He knew, like I did, that music was of my soul. The sound itself wasn't important.

Music made me happy.

But when I opened my violin case, my happiness vanished.

My journal was gone.

The one where I'd scribbled Jason's name. Over and over again.

Jason was a freshman at summer music camp. He was naturally tan, just like me, and the only openly gay kid I'd ever seen. Until I met him, I'd never known a real gay kid.

I'd never actually talked to Jason. I'd been too scared. But I'd liked his smile because it reminded me of another smile, a smile from my dreams. I didn't know whose smile it was, only that it warmed me, and made me happy.

Ever since then, thinking of Jason brought me closer to that smile.

So I'd written his name over and over again in my journal. It may not have been such a big deal, if it weren't for the millions of hearts I'd drawn around his name, and the fact that Jason wasn't a name that could be either a boy or a girl.

Absentmindedly, I reached under my shirt to feel the scraped skin on my side. This afternoon, Jimmy had shoved me against my locker and called me queerboy. Normally, that would have made today pretty much like any other day.

Only today Jimmy's smirk had been brighter, and he'd sounded more sadistic and ecstatic than usual. Now I knew why.

I'd kept my journal in my violin case because the band room was supposed to be locked. But Jimmy had found it anyway. He'd stolen it. And read it.

Panic exploded in my chest and my fingers started twitching madly.

I knew what Sammy thought of boys who liked boys. Last summer, just before I left for music camp, we saw Marcus Calvin holding hands with another guy at Mike's Burgers. Sammy had shuddered and said they disgusted him and gave him the creeps.

He dragged me out of there so quick that he didn't even finish his shake. Like he was scared we might catch something from them.

I'd lived in fear ever since.

Because all I could think of was, what would happen if he knew that I was just like them?

Jimmy called me gay, homo, and queer because he thought they were insults.

But Jimmy's words weren't the ones that cut me the deepest. Mine were.

Every time he called me gay, I lied and told him it wasn't true.

Only I wasn't lying to Jimmy. I was lying to myself. I kept hoping that if I said it often enough, it would stop being true. And then I wouldn't have to worry about Sammy finding out and disowning me as his best friend.

But every time that lie rolled off my tongue, my soul cringed. How could I ever hope to grow into my ears and into my soul if in the deep, dark recesses of me I hated who I was?

Mom had taken away orchestra and my clubhouse. Sammy was all I had left.

And Jimmy was going to take him away too.

By Monday, every kid in school would know. Including Sammy. I wouldn't be able to hide any longer.

I thought about telling Sammy right then and getting it over with. Yet if I said nothing, I could have my friend for two more days. After that, I could go hide somewhere where nobody could find me. Not even Sammy. Mice were good at hiding, especially small ones with big ears.

"Dude, you gonna play or what?" Sammy asked indignantly.

I should have told him then. But I couldn't. Rick was right. I was gutless.

Suddenly, a strange peace came over me. My secret was out. I was going to lose Sammy. I was going to lose everything. I had nothing left to lose.

It was actually a huge relief. I even smiled at Sammy as I picked up my violin.

Sammy grinned back with his deepest, most dimpled grin. When he did, his smile made me think of that other smile, the one in my dreams.

It was a good moment.

I was in my clubhouse. With my best friend. I had my violin in my hand. I could feel my father's presence. And in my mind I saw the smile that I loved, more vividly than I ever had.

It was a perfect moment in time. A moment of love, and hope, and beauty. And it was mine. Nobody could take it from me. No matter what happened.

I took that moment, froze it, and tucked it away in my soul to keep forever.

And as I did, my soul played a new song, one I'd heard long ago, in a dream of my father.

It was the purest music my soul had ever played and I closed my eyes and let it carry me away. But all too soon a strange sound poked at my brain and forced me back.

When I opened my eyes, the first thing I noticed was that my orange-and-red rock was glowing brightly.

Then I saw Sammy. His eyes were so wide I thought his eyeballs would pop. His mouth was moving and his hands were gesturing madly at something behind me.

That's when I realized that Sammy was the sound poking at my brain.

"Jacob! Jacob! Look!"

I turned around and immediately forgot about the glowing rock. In fact, I forgot about everything else that had happened.

Because the tree in the middle of my clubhouse was shimmering, the way water ripples when you throw a stone into a lake.

"What's happening?" My voice sounded tinny, and distant.

"I have no idea."

I suppose we both thought that if we stared long enough, it would stop. But it didn't.

Eventually curiosity won out. Sammy edged over to the tree and gingerly stretched out his right hand.

But when Sammy reached the tree in the middle of my clubhouse, the clubhouse that I built with my father exactly eight years ago to the day, my violin slipped through my fingers and clattered to the floor.

Sammy's fingers didn't touch the tree. They disappeared right into it.

ONE SMALL STEP

I KNEW THAT trees were not supposed to shimmer, and that hands were not supposed to disappear into trees. Even so, seeing Sammy's hand disappear into a shimmering tree did not seem as bizarre to me as it should have.

Sammy withdrew his hand from the tree and wriggled his fingers. When he saw that they were all there he broke into a huge grin.

"Wow! How cool is that?!" He said.

"Very cool," I murmured. "We should go through."

My words must have sounded as odd to Sammy as they did to me because Sammy looked at me like I'd gone crazy. Crazy in a way he kind of liked.

"You want to?" he asked.

"Yeah, I do." In fact, I couldn't remember ever having wanted to do anything quite as badly as I wanted to step through that tree.

"Well, why not?" Sammy grinned. "I'll go first, and you wait for a minute. If it's cool, I'll come back and get you, okay?"

"Okay."

Sammy stepped towards the tree.

I blinked.

When I opened my eyes he was gone.

I should have been terrified. And I was nervous. But mostly, I was exhilarated. The tree had awakened something long dormant within me.

I couldn't wait for Sammy. I had to know now. So I took a deep breath, squeezed my eyes shut, and leapt.

It wasn't what happened that surprised me, it was what didn't. I did not bounce off the tree with a bloody nose. My body did not dematerialize into a gazillion pieces and then rematerialize. And I did not squeeze through an exciting, tubular wormhole.

One minute, I was in my clubhouse. The next, my foot was touching down on something crunchy. Other than that, and a tingle so faint that I barely noticed it, I'd felt nothing at all.

I was actually a bit disappointed. Until I opened my eyes.

Sammy glanced at me but said nothing. And I quickly saw why.

We were standing at the edge of a small clearing. Above us, a dozen moons loomed large, and pinpoints of light glittered across a magnificent night sky that bore no resemblance to Earth's night sky.

And I realized we were not on Earth.

Just as that realization dawned, we heard a cracking of branches and rustling of leaves behind us. Sammy and I stared into the forest, neither of us daring to breathe, certain that we were about to become some monster's late-night snack.

But whatever it was must have decided we didn't smell so tasty after all. The noises quickly faded until the only remaining sound was the thunder of our pounding hearts.

Once we recovered from our brush with being eaten alive, we dragged our eyes from the glorious sky to take a closer look at our surroundings.

The trees were a vibrant mix of colors—purple, green, orange, yellow, red, and just about every color in between.

A fuzzy orange starfish-like thing dangled from the branch of the closest tree. I reached up to explore its texture. It was warm and soft and purred beneath my fingers.

"Wow," Sammy whistled. His eyes were huge. Mine were probably even bigger.

"Yeah," I agreed.

A raspy, sarcastic voice shattered the moment. "'Wow.' 'Yeah.' Oh boy, how *brilliant*."

My heart skipped a beat. From the look on Sammy's face, his did too. Had the monster decided we looked tasty after all?

"Well, well, well, what have we got here?" The voice sounded less than two feet away. But despite the bright moons, we couldn't see anyone.

"Who said that?" Sammy asked.

"Why, I did of course," the voice crooned.

Sammy laughed nervously as if he thought he might be hearing things. "Dude, you heard that, right?"

"Yeah, I heard it."

Suddenly a rapid clickety-clack noise started up directly in front of us. It droned on for a few moments, then stopped as abruptly as it had started.

"Unbelievable," the voice muttered with an exaggerated sigh. "After all these years, he doesn't bother to come back himself. Nooo. Instead, he sends a couple of kiddies through. Well, I don't find it funny."

Sammy spun in a circle and looked the tree up and down. "Who doesn't come back? And who are you? Where are you?"

A ferret popped out onto the limb in front of us, so close I could have touched it had I not chosen the safer option of dashing to safety behind Sammy's elbow.

"I'm right here, Buttercup." The ferret lumbered closer and waved a paw. "Can you see me now?"

Sammy searched around the tree to see who was really talking, leaving me dangerously exposed, I couldn't help but notice.

"You can look all you want, young biped." The ferret continued along the limb. "But I'm right—" He stopped just in front of me and whispered, in a voice that sounded strangely in awe, "You must be Jacob."

"What?" It came out as a squeak.

"I saaaaid. Youuuuuuu. Muuuuuust. Beeeeee. Jacob."

"How do you know my name?"

"What? Didn't he tell you about me?"

"Didn't *who* tell me about you?"

The ferret drummed his razor-sharp claws against his pointy, and even sharper-looking, teeth. The rapid clickety-clack was even noisier than it had been the first time.

"Oh boy, but why am I surprised? Typical humans. Never think of anyone but themselves. That's the problem with underdeveloped brains. Still I would have thought he'd, just when you think—"

"Who are you talking about?" Sammy asked.

The ferret turned to me and snapped, "Prantos. You know, Jacob, your father? Supposedly my friend, but I guess I was wrong about that, hmpf."

"My father? Prantos?"

Never in my life had I heard my father's name uttered out loud by anyone. Not even by my mother. Especially not by my mother.

"Yippy. You can repeat me. Yes, your father, Prantos."

The ferret paced back and forth along the limb. The more agitated he got, the louder his tooth-drumming sounded.

"Look, why don't you scamper back and tell Daddyo he's had his fun and if he wouldn't mind, could he please come? I really don't have the time to deal with younglings."

My knees went weak and I stumbled into Sammy. For suddenly, I had a vision of my father, standing in front of this very tree with a ferret wrapped around his neck.

And when I took in a long, deep breath, I could smell him. And hear his laughter. My father had been here, and I had been here with him.

Sammy wrapped his arm around me to keep me from falling. "You okay, Jakey?"

I nodded and managed to get my feet back under me before I looked up and choked out the painful words. "My dad died eight years ago."

The ferret halted in his tracks. His eyes grew wide. "I am sorry, Jacob. I did not know."

"Come on, Jacob," Sammy said. "Let's get away from this talking ferret."

"I am not a ferret, my little nursling, I am Koopf."

"What's a Koopf?" Sammy asked.

"Koopfs are beings of superior intellect." The not-a-ferret spoke as if it should be obvious. Then he turned to me. "Allow me to introduce myself. My name is Bringelkoopf, and I already know you are Jacob, but who is that one? And more importantly, why is he here?"

"His name is Sammy, he's my best and only friend."

"What do you mean, 'your only friend'? I, too, am your friend, and therefore that young cub is not your only friend."

"My friend? We only just met, and as far as I can tell, you aren't very nice." I'd never spoken to anyone like that before. It startled me. From the look on Sammy's face, it startled him too.

"I was a close friend of your father's, and now that he has passed—may his soul rest in peace—well, I am your friend. Now I must take you to Michael."

"Who's Michael?" I asked.

"Someone you need to see," he said. With that, he floated down and bounded off, clearly expecting us to follow without question.

Sammy and I stood rooted to the spot and stared after him.

Bringelkoopf stopped and turned back. "Aren't you coming, Jacob?"

Sammy and I looked at each other. We had no idea what we'd heard crashing through the trees earlier, but whatever it was it had sounded a lot bigger than Bringelkoopf. Did we really want to remain alone in this strange place?

It never occurred to us to simply step back through the tree. And following Bringelkoopf seemed like the least bad of the bad options swirling through our heads.

So we followed the sarcastic not-a-ferret into a strange forest on a strange planet that was quite obviously not Earth.

I savored the smell of the air with every breath and every step.

It was strangely familiar, similar to the strange musky scent of my orange-and-red rock.

I didn't realize it, but a part of me knew exactly what it was. It was the smell of home.

CONNECTIONS

AVERAGE. THAT WAS my first impression of Michael. It lasted about five seconds.

After dragging us on a hike as long and miserable as a full day of school, Bringelkoopf had left us in what looked like the middle of nowhere while he slithered off through the tangled purple-and-orange overgrowth of a huge and gnarly tree.

Just when my overactive imagination began to wonder if we were about to become Michael's nightly snack, the tangled mess around the gnarly tree parted, and a man—not a monster, but an amazingly average-looking man—emerged.

He wasn't tall or short, fat or skinny, but somewhere in between. His hair was black, long enough that it wasn't short, with enough of a wave that it wasn't straight. You know, average.

But that's where the average stopped.

As he glided towards us, trailing a bright red cloak, his legs flowed like smooth silk beneath him while the rest of him appeared to be merely coming along for the ride.

When he reached us, his face lit up with the most extraordinary smile I'd ever seen.

"Jacob, Sammy," he boomed in the deepest and friendliest voice in all the universe. "Welcome!"

That's when I noticed his eyes. They were the most phenomenal thing about him. They glittered with pinpoints of bursting light, radiating a warmth and kindness that made me feel happy and safe.

I realized then that there was absolutely nothing average about Michael.

As I stared into his sparkling eyes, I again felt something stir within me that told me none of this was as strange as it ought to be.

"It is so good to see you, Jacob," he said.

He shook my hand in a way that no adult ever had, as one man to another. Then he led us, quite literally, into the huge and gnarly tree—which just happened to be his front door.

Michael's underground cabin was as not-average as its owner. And not just because of the sarcastic not-a-ferret curled up on the table.

For one thing, the walls were decorated with hundreds of purring orange starfish-like things, filling the cabin with a bright but soothingly warm glow.

For another, the floor was covered with green, spongy stuff that just begged us to toss off our shoes and curl our toes in it, which Sammy did the minute we entered.

A lot of people would have been upset by a strange kid going barefoot in their home. Michael merely chuckled. "You should give it a try, Jacob. Your feet will thank you."

I'd just walked more in one night than I had in an entire year. I tore off my shoes and socks almost as fast as Sammy had. Michael was right. My feet did thank me.

But the most awesome thing about Michael's cabin was the humongous stone fireplace in the middle. Sammy and I were both drawn to it like magnets.

Sammy, because of the mouthwatering aroma of cinnamon, apples and something else rising from the stew simmering on its hearth.

I, because of the red-hot crackling fire and the enticing scent of burning wood.

The last time I'd seen a real fire had been on a camping trip with Mom and Rick. Rick had tried to teach me to roast a marshmallow. On my first try I'd dropped the marshmallow, and my hand along with it, into the fire. My right hand tingled at the memory.

Mom hadn't let me near a fire since. But it was the best memory I had of my mom and step-dad together. Because they'd spent the rest of the night roasting my marshmallows for me.

My mouth watered at the memory. Or perhaps it was at the smell of Michael's stew. Either way, staring into the dancing flames made me hungry and happy.

"You boys hungry?" Michael asked.

"Starving," Sammy said.

"Me too," I agreed.

With a meaningful glance at our hands, Michael nodded at the door in the corner. "You could both do with a bit of a clean-up first. Wash-cubbies are in the dens."

Sammy and I looked at our hands.

I groaned.

Although we were both dusty from our trek through the woods, my hands were filthier than Sammy's. There had been so many colorful leaves with delightful textures to explore.

What Michael called dens were actually seven heavenly-cozy bedrooms. Each one with a unique personality. There were so many nooks and crannies that we could have explored for hours.

If we hadn't been so hungry.

I made it back to the hearth room before Sammy did. I wasn't scared to be alone with Michael, but even so I felt strangely abandoned without Sammy.

Michael stirred his stew quietly and let me study him. He reminded me of what I'd always thought a grandfather would be like.

My fingers twitched as I waited for Sammy. Remembering the feel of the orange starfish-like thing on the tree, I wandered to the wall and set my fingers on one of them.

It purred, just like the one in the forest. Though for some reason, this one tickled more.

"What are these?" I asked Michael.

"They're called strictors. I've always used them, but most people use oil and wood."

"What do you use them for?"

Michael laughed and gestured around the room. "Light. We don't have electricity on Portalia, Jacob."

At his words, my heart quivered.

"Portalia." I rolled the name off my tongue over and over again. I relished the way it tasted, odd, yet right, like warm apple pie.

When Sammy returned, Michael clapped his hands together and chivvied us to the table. "Time to eat," he said, with an eager glint in his eye.

Bringelkoopf perked up and the three of us sat together and watched as Michael dazzled us with his stew serving ritual.

He brandished his stir spoon as if he were a conductor conducting an orchestra and the spoon his baton. With every swish and swoop, he circled his head above the stew and inhaled deeply to savor its newly released aromas.

When his lungs could take in no more, he gave the pot a final, flourishing stir and, with a satisfied nod, let out a long contented sigh.

Setting the spoon carefully to the side, as if it was an irreplaceable treasure, he glided to the cupboard and swept up four mugs.

Then he floated back to the fireplace, scooped up a ladle full of orange mush and, pausing just long enough to cast a wink in our direction, filled the first mug with an elaborate swoosh. In the flash of an eye, he whisked that mug to the side, scooped up the next one, and repeated the entire process.

When he'd filled the last mug, he sent three of them sailing across the table to us. They slid to a smooth halt directly beneath our noses.

Seemingly out of nowhere, a loaf of bread appeared in Michael's hand and landed on the table with a soft plunk.

Sammy immediately tore off a chunk and dunked it in his stew.

"Not surprised he'd be a glutton," Bringelkoopf said, greedily clutching his own chunk.

When I made no move to eat, Michael looked crushed. For a fraction of a second. Then his eyes lit up and he let out a hearty laugh. "We don't use utensils on Portalia, Jacob. That's what the bread is for."

I was still hesitant. Mom was a stickler for table manners.

Michael slapped my back. "Go on, Jacob, dig in, enjoy."

It's not that I wasn't hungry, I was. But I didn't reach for the bread because I was hungry. I reached for it because Michael looked like it would break his heart if I didn't.

I quickly discovered that the chewy bread was far better than a spoon. And that the cinnamon, apples and something else-flavored orange mush was, well, out of this world. I doubted Michael would ever again have to nag me to dig in.

"Something to drink?" Michael rubbed his hands together so eagerly that I wondered how long it had been since he'd had such ravenous company.

"Yes, please," I said.

Sammy said nothing. Instead, he nodded and gave Michael a thumbs-up. It turned out that Sammy's ability to talk around a mouthful did not apply to liquid food.

Michael appeared to take Sammy's hamster-like food-stuffed cheeks as a compliment.

Almost as quickly as the bread had appeared, two mugs of bubbly, vibrant purple liquid arrived in front of us.

"This is frinkle," Michael said with a note of near reverence. "It's my favorite."

Frinkle is hot, liquid peanut butter cup goodness in a mug. After one sip I decided frinkle was my favorite too. It was the best thing that had ever happened to my tongue. It soothed my body all the way from my parched mouth to my blistered feet.

With food in his belly, Sammy was back to his usual inquisitive self. "So, is this like a parallel universe or something?"

"Yes, Sammy," Michael said. "Portalia, and each of her twelve moons, exists within a parallel universe."

"What's a parallel universe?" I asked.

"Please tell me you're joking," Bringelkoopf muttered. He quickly wilted beneath a stern glance from Michael.

"A parallel universe is a universe that exists in the same place as another universe, but in a different dimension," Michael explained.

That was not even remotely helpful.

Michael cupped his hands together. "Parallel universes are like different channels on a television. The television is where we are. Earth is on one channel, and Portalia on another. They are both in the same place, just on different channels."

For a split second, I almost got it. Then Michael spoke again.

"But it isn't quite that simple." His eyes twinkled with a mischievous glint.

I groaned. "Of course not. That would be too convenient."

Sammy giggled at my reaction and choked on his frinkle.

Michael laughed too, but not at me. His laugh, like his voice, was friendly. "Even most Portalians don't know about parallel universes, Jacob. But because of Portalia's purpose...."

He drifted off briefly, then shook his head and continued. "Humans see things as being up, down, forward, backward. But a universe is more complicated than that. It isn't flat like a piece of paper. It's shaped in a way you humans cannot seem to understand."

I was about to ask him why he referred to us as "you humans." But when I looked into his eyes with their pinpoints of light that sparkled like stars, I realized I already knew that the man sitting across from me wasn't human. In fact, I'd known it all along. I just hadn't realized it.

Michael gave me an all-knowing wink, then pulled out two sheets of paper, like the bread and frinkle, from seemingly nowhere.

He held the first sheet up. "Let's call this Earth's universe."

He divided the second sheet into four pieces and selected one. "And let's call this one Portalia's universe, the parallel universe."

"Earth's universe is much bigger than Portalia's," I said.

"Yes."

"So how can they be in the same place?"

"Ah, that's just the question. Only some parts are in the same place."

Michael folded the Earth's universe paper lengthwise, back and forth on itself in one-inch sections like a paper fan, then placed it on the table.

It looked like lots of mountain peaks side by side.

He set the Portalia universe paper on top of it and sat back to watch me.

The Portalia universe covered the entire Earth universe, but only touched it at the peaks.

Sammy figured it out right away. He looked fit to explode with excitement. Only the kind but stern shake of Michael's head kept him from blurting out the answer.

My brain itched. I scratched my head, but it didn't help. It never did. "So, the Portalia universe only connects with the Earth universe in certain places?"

"Yes." Michael beamed as if I'd just said something brilliant.

He unfolded Earth's universe and drew two dots, four inches apart. "Now, if you wanted to travel from one dot to another, say from one solar system to another solar system in Earth's universe, it would take you thousands of years, right?"

Science was Sammy's thing, not mine. But I had no reason to think Michael was asking me a trick question. "I guess so," I said.

He refolded Earth's universe and set it back on the table. Now the two dots, each on a mountain peak, were side by side, nearly touching each other.

He placed Portalia's universe back on top of Earth's. "But what if you could pop out of Earth and onto Portalia, travel a mere hop, skip and a jump, and go back to Earth's universe. How long would it take you then?"

It was more than Sammy could handle. He bolted from his seat. "Instead of taking hundreds and hundreds and thousands and thousands of years, traveling at the speed of light, which we can't do anyway, we could go from one solar system to another in a year or something. Not even traveling at the speed of light, which, you know, isn't possible."

Sammy stopped to catch his breath. He grinned so wide it buried his dimples. "Dude, you could be that intergalactic musician dude you've always wanted to be, you really could. Your father really did give you the stars. How cool is that?"

Michael nodded. "Just like with people, Earth and Portalia have complementary strengths that, if combined, would allow them both to reach their full potential. If Earth's technology were to be combined with Portalia's ability to connect with vast numbers of solar systems and galaxies, there would be no place in the universe humans could not reach."

Bringelkoopf stirred then, and he and Michael exchanged an odd glance.

I was too thunderstruck to register it, though. Michael had just told me that my lifelong dream wasn't a foolish fantasy.

Michael scratched Bringelkoopf behind the ears and gave me a moment to let that sink in.

"I'm not a pet," Bringelkoopf grumbled. But he could not hide a contented purr as he leaned into Michael's fingers.

"Earth's strength is her technological development." Michael continued petting the not-a-ferret but he swiveled his eyes to mine. "And Portalia's is her music."

A cold chill crept up my spine. I tugged out my pockets so my fingers could pluck them.

Michael's eyes remained warm, but the sparkles shifted to dark swirls. He leaned toward me with such intensity that a yelp of surprise caught in my throat.

"Jacob, how did you open the port? How did you get here?"

"I don't know," I told him. And I didn't.

"Tell me what you were doing, just before it happened?"

"I was playing my violin...."

For the first time since the tree started shimmering, I remembered the empty violin case. Panic surged. But then the smile that I love came to my mind. Just like it had in the clubhouse, right before I played my violin, when Sammy had smiled at me.

The panic evaporated. For the smile warmed me and made me happy, like it always did. I remembered the moment that I'd captured, when I'd been thinking about the smile. It had been a moment of love and hope and beauty. And it was mine to keep forever.

"Jacob?" Michael's voice broke into my thoughts.

Reluctantly, I tucked the moment back away.

"All I know," I told him, "is that my soul decided to play a new song. I closed my eyes and got lost in it. I wasn't paying attention to anything else. When I opened my eyes, the tree was shimmering."

I was not prepared for what I saw next.

Michael shook his head with a soft smile in that weird way adults sometimes do when they are very proud of you.

But Bringelkoopf perplexed me even more. His face gleamed with admiration and a note of reverence was evident in his voice. "You did it without even trying?"

Their reactions stunned me. I was the ordinary kid with extraordinary dreams and not a lick of talent to speak of. Unless you counted my talent for being below average at everything I did, no matter how hard I tried. I was definitely not the guy you stared at the way they were, like I was a wonderful gift they'd been waiting for their entire lives.

"So, how did we get here?" I asked.

"You opened a portal, Jacob, a doorway between Earth and Portalia," Michael said.

That confused me even more. Opening a portal sounded suspiciously like something that would require a talent or skill of some sort.

"But how?" Sammy asked.

Sammy would have to wait for his answer. For when Michael spoke, though his words shocked me to my very core, they had nothing to do with how I'd opened a portal.

"Jacob, did you know that your father had a brother?"

I knew nothing of the sort. In fact, I knew just the opposite. One of the very few things I'd managed to drag from my mom about my father was that he was an orphan and an only child.

Except, apparently, he wasn't.

I was too stunned to even wonder why Mom would have lied about that.

My father had a brother. I had an uncle. My fingers began tweaking a section of my fast-dwindling pocket fabric into oblivion.

Michael continued in a calm and soothing voice, like you would use with a skittish animal, or, in my case, a frightened mouse. "His name is Grolfshin. He's your father's younger brother."

Michael sandwiched my hands gently between his. I was surprised at how soft they were. Michael struck me as the kind of man who liked to work with his hands. I'd expected him to have hands with calluses. But then, I would have expected him to have a cheerful smile on his face too. After all, he was telling me I had an uncle.

"Jacob, Portalia is a kingdom. Do you know what that means?"

I shrugged. "That Portalia is run by a King?"

"Yes. That's exactly what it means."

"Okay?"

"Jacob, your father, is... was Portalia's King."

A voice in the back of my brain told me that Michael had just said something important, something that was going to change my life forever. But I couldn't quite figure out what it was.

Sammy had no such difficulty. "That would make Jacob the King," he said.

"What?" I squeaked.

"And yet again, my brilliant cherub dazzles everyone with his quick wit." Bringelkoopf had obviously recovered from his dangerous bout of gleaming admiration.

"After you were born," Michael said, "your father asked Grolfshin to watch over Portalia while he went to Earth. Grolfshin loved your father very much. He was very devoted to him."

"Yeah, right, devoted as a leech," Bringelkoopf spat.

Michael's eyebrow twitched. "Your father came back every year during Portal Week. Then eight years ago he disappeared. Grolfshin has been acting King ever since. He does his best, I know he does—"

"The best for himself." Bringelkoopf thumped the floor with his tail. He started pacing and drumming his claws against his teeth.

Michael glared at him briefly. "But power is a great temptation, Jacob, and many a man has been lured astray by it."

"So, my uncle is the King." My brain stumbled about in a daze.

"No, Jacob, you are Prantos' only son. You are the rightful King of Portalia, if you choose to accept that duty and follow your destiny. That is a choice only you can make. But now that you are on Portalia, your place is not here with me, but at the castle..." Michael dropped his gaze. "...with your uncle. Tomorrow you shall meet him."

"Does he know about me?"

Sammy had been watching the agitated not-a-ferret, and he had an altogether different concern. "He isn't going to be exactly happy to see Jacob, is he?"

"I cannot say how he will feel, Sammy, but I imagine he will be very surprised."

"That is the tiniest little understatement," Bringelkoopf said.

"And yes, Jacob," Michael went on, "he knows about you."

"How come he never came to visit me?" Uncles visited, right?

"He cannot open a portal." Michael smiled wistfully. "If he could, maybe things would have been different."

With that, he rose abruptly. "It's almost morning. You boys need your sleep. You have a long day ahead."

I suddenly realized I was very, very tired.

The last thought that crossed my mind as I fell onto the bed, which could have been a cement slab for all I cared, was that Michael said I had an uncle, and I was going to meet him.

But he'd said something else too. Something important. And I couldn't shake a nagging feeling that my life was about to change forever, and that it had something to do with me being the heir to my father's throne.

THE JOURNEY BEGINS

SAMMY WAS ELBOW DEEP in food by the time I got to the table.

He had on bright Portalian clothes just like I did. I wondered if he'd put up a fight. On Earth, he wouldn't have been caught dead in anything so colorful.

Sammy grinned when he saw me. He looked me up and down and plucked at his own bright orange shirt. "Well, at least now I know where you get your fashion sense. Hate to admit it, but these things are comfy."

Vibrant colors have always soothed and comforted me. My irritation at the obnoxiously cheerful not-a-ferret for jolting me out of a deep sleep had evaporated immediately when Michael set the brightly colored clothes on the foot of my bed.

The orange pants and the puffy red shirt were even more comfortable than they looked. They were made from a sturdy fabric that had a delightfully soothing texture to it. Best of all, they had huge pockets for my fingers to tweak.

Nothing had ever felt more right on my body.

If it weren't for the panic that had my stomach on the verge of throwing up, I would have been on cloud nine. But today I was going to meet my long lost uncle. All I could think of was, what would he think of me? Would he be as thrilled to meet me as I was to meet him?

Brunch consisted of apple shaped yellow things, orange shaped purple things, banana shaped green things, and fluorescent lime-green syrup. It smelled like taste bud heaven and my stomach finally gave in and agreed not to revolt.

Even in my nerve-wracked state I couldn't help but giggle at the sight of Michael greedily licking his fingers clean.

My mom would have had a conniption fit. Mom. For a horrifying second I wondered if she'd discovered we were missing. Then I reminded myself that since she refused to set foot in the clubhouse, she'd only notice we were gone if we weren't back for Sunday dinner.

I wondered if Mom knew about Portalia. But she would have told me if I had an uncle, wouldn't she? I suppose I should have given that more thought, but I do not do my best thinking in the morning.

Sammy, on the other hand, does his best thinking twenty-four hours a day. He spoke around nonstop mouthfuls of food with his customary finesse. "So, how did Bringelkoopf know we were coming? Can you tell when someone opens a port?"

Michael slurped up a blob of lemon foam. "No, I cannot tell when someone opens a port. It isn't magic, Sammy. Bringelkoopf met you because he was waiting for Prantos."

Sammy paused to display his charming, mischievous grin. "He's been waiting for eight years? No wonder he's so sarcastic."

That tickled Michael's funny bone something fierce.

He roared with laughter, slapping the table so enthusiastically that it rattled and shook, lobbing food in all directions. For a second I feared there'd been an earthquake. But when Michael finally succeeded in bringing his outburst under control, the table settled quickly. The only remaining tremors were the waves of laughter that continued to wash over him.

Sammy, with his lightning-fast reflexes, had managed to prevent his food, and his alone, from taking flight. From the absentminded way Michael picked the rest of the catapulted food off the floor, I suspected this was far from the first time he'd scattered a meal with his laughter.

"Actually, Bringelkoopf has always been sarcastic."

"I don't appreciate that," Bringelkoopf grunted.

Michael's voice was surprisingly gentle. "No, you only like being on the other end, don't you, my good friend." He reached out to scratch the not-a-ferret. "I'm sorry."

Bringelkoopf pulled away, but not before Michael managed to get in a few scratches.

"Bringelkoopf hasn't been there all this time, Sammy. Just during Portal Week, and only at the times that he and Prantos agreed upon."

"What's Portal Week?" Sammy asked. "You mentioned it last night too."

"Portal Week is the only time of the year that portals can be opened between worlds."

"So, it's Portal Week right now?" I asked.

"Yes," Michael said, with an odd tinge of sadness in his voice. "Yes, it is."

"So, when Portal Week is over, there won't be any way to move between Earth and Portalia again until next year?" Sammy asked.

"That's correct, Sammy."

Michael got up from the table with a reluctant sigh. "If you're to make it before sundown, you three should leave soon."

"We *three*?" Sammy asked.

"I don't like it either, Buttercup," Bringelkoopf said. "A day with infant bipeds is not my idea of an even remotely enjoyable day."

"You're not coming?" I asked Michael.

"It's better if I don't. But Bringelkoopf can hide in the shoulder flap of your shirt. Nobody will know he's there, and he can... help... if you need it."

"So, what do I do? Walk up, knock on the door and say 'Hi, Uncle, surprise, it's me'?"

"I suggest you have the village messenger boy deliver a letter first. It would be too much of a shock otherwise."

"Might give him a heart attack." Bringelkoopf sounded almost hopeful.

Michael pointedly ignored his furry friend. "Little Roland Harkins runs even faster than Sammy eats." He gave Sammy an affectionate wink. "Your letter should arrive thirty minutes before you do. But before you go, Jacob.... I do not want to interfere, but...."

Sammy raised his eyebrows. "What do you mean you don't want to interfere? You obviously think he needs to be careful about something."

"Yes, I do." Michael studied his hands and shook his head at a painful memory. "Grolfshin has changed, Jacob. Your father's disappearance wounded him very deeply."

Bringelkoopf sputtered in protest, but Michael placed his hand on the not-a-ferret's head and spoke, in a voice laced with pain, "Please do not take this from me, my friend."

His words made no sense to me, but they must have to Bringelkoopf. Because the not-a-ferret who, two seconds earlier had been sulking like a toddler denied his rightful candy, nodded and even rubbed up against Michael's fingers to allow a suspiciously pet-like scratching.

"Jacob," Michael said, "you cannot, under any circumstances, tell Grolfshin that you opened a port."

"But what if he asks how I got here? I mean, he will, won't he?"

"Of course he will, but I suggest you be cautious, and not tell him the truth right away."

"You mean lie?"

"I would suggest that you tell him a different story, so that you leave your options open. But I can't tell you what to do, Jacob. You must make your own decisions."

Sammy got up and paced even though there was still food on the table. I'd never seen him so serious. "He's right, Jacob. You could be a threat to your uncle, since technically you could take his place."

"Yeah, but I don't want to. I mean, look at me. I haven't even grown into my ears yet."

"But he won't know that, Jakey. And if he knows about Earth, and Earth's technology, and he finds out that you can get him there....Look, once you get to know him, if it turns out he's really a stand-up guy, you can tell him the truth. If he really cares about you, he'll understand."

Sammy folded his arms and turned to Michael. "So, what's your plan?"

* * *

Portalia in the sunlight was a rainbow version of the Garden of Eden. I noticed that many trees, not just the orange ones, had furry, humming strictors.

The ground was damp from a late night rain. The sun was bright and the sky empty of clouds. I tilted my head back to soak in the heat. I was going to meet my uncle, and I smiled.

Bringelkoopf saw my smile, and he and Michael exchanged worried glances.

As Bringelkoopf tucked himself under the puffy shoulder flap of my shirt, I found myself thinking how odd it was that I'd already learned to read the expressions on his face. Strangely, it did not occur to me to wonder why the expression in question was one of worry.

Once Bringelkoopf was settled to Michael's satisfaction, Sammy prodded the back flap and shook his head in wonder. "It's like he's not even there."

"Poke that finger this way, just once more," came Bringelkoopf's muffled growl, "and I'll show you how not-here I am."

I laughed, and with that, we headed off to meet my uncle.

I have often wondered what the fate of my people would have been, if the small boy who had not yet grown into his ears had taken a moment to wonder about the worry on the faces of a wise old man and his furry companion.

I think I would have returned to the safety of the clubhouse I'd built with my father. I might have even helped Rick board it up. And in so doing, I would have unknowingly sealed the fate of millions.

For Michael hadn't told me about one decision that was not mine to make. The choice as to whether or not I would hold the fate of many people in my hands had been made for me. At the moment of my birth.

TIES THAT BIND

WE'D JUST CRESTED the third hill since Talarkin village when we saw it on the distant horizon. A very real, very big, and very bright orange-and-red castle.

A flurry of dust, with the messenger boy in the middle, sped up the hill towards us. We were still staring speechlessly when Roland Harkins zipped by on his way back to Talarkin village. "Hi, bye," he hollered as he passed.

I'd been skeptical when I first met Roland Harkins. He was half my size and his legs were like twigs. But the moment I'd placed my letter into his hands he'd taken off in a blur and was out of sight before the dust had settled.

We were just over halfway to the castle and he was already on his way back.

Which meant my uncle knew I was coming.

Suddenly, I began to fret about all the pesky things I'd been conveniently ignoring. Like the fact that everybody felt I needed a cover story to explain to my uncle how I'd gotten here.

And what if Sammy was right, which, I had to admit, he pretty much always was? What if Grolfshin thought I was a threat and threw me in a dungeon for the rest of my life? All self-respecting castles had dungeons, didn't they? And that very big castle definitely looked self-respecting enough to have a dungeon. A colorful one maybe, but a dungeon nonetheless.

* * *

I got my first glimpse of my uncle when we passed through the castle's purple and orange main gate.

He was leaning casually against the front door, tapping my letter against his palm and watching our approach. He wore a magnificent purple robe that billowed gently in the breeze. His skin, like my father's, was a shade darker than mine, and he had curly black hair and pokey-out ears just like me.

My hands twitched in the secrecy of my pockets. I noticed that his fingers flicked too.

"I think somebody's nervous," Bringelkoopf said. It took me a minute to realize he was talking about my uncle, not me. That did nothing to ease my anxiety.

But as soon as we reached the bottom of the steps, Grolfshin burst into a grin, trotted down and swept me up into a bear hug. "Jacob. Oh, Jacob," he said.

And just like that, all my worries vanished. He felt and smelled just like my father. I wrapped my arms around him and held on as tight as I could. I was in heaven and never wanted to let go.

I could tell he felt the same way. He sobbed quietly into my hair, and it was a long time before he finally set me down to get a better look.

"I cannot believe it—it truly *is* you. Oh Jacob, it is so very good to see you again."

"Again?"

"Oh, you wouldn't remember," he said with a dismissive wave of his hand. "You were so little, you came just up to my knee." He grinned and ran his fingers through my hair. "Eleven years later and here you are."

He glanced at Sammy as if he'd only just noticed him. "Grolfshin Prios. And you are?"

"Sammy. It's a pleasure to meet you, sir." Sammy held out his hand.

"Sammy's my friend," I added at Grolfshin's dubious frown.

"Ah, wonderful. Of course, any friend of my nephew's is always welcome." Grolfshin smiled, but maneuvered away without shaking Sammy's hand. "Come then, we have so much catching up to do."

He threw his arm around me, earning me a sharp and painful complaint from my hidden furry friend, and led us up the steps. When he swung open the castle's heavy front door, he stepped aside to give us a view. Were it not for the hand he kept on my elbow, I think I would have done a face-plant on the red slate floor at the sight.

The entryway alone was bigger than the Archer Middle School auditorium. On either side, magnificent staircases with polished wood banisters spiraled upwards.

But it was the floor-to-vaulted-ceiling sculptured wood walls that literally took my breath away. They were inlaid with panoramic scenes of mountains and oceans and picturesque stories depicting unicorns, dragons, eagles, and men in flowing robes.

It was the most spectacular thing I'd ever seen.

"Welcome home," Grolfshin said.

"Is the whole thing made from one piece of wood?" Sammy asked.

Grolfshin laughed. "Oh, goodness no. I don't think a big enough tree exists. But even so, nobody has ever been able to tell where one piece ends and another begins."

Sammy arched his eyebrow. "Nobody?"

"Who knows? Maybe you'll be the first."

"Maybe."

As Sammy began searching for the hidden seam, Grolfshin led me on a more personal tour of the walls.

He jabbed his thumb at a massive willow tree and nodded towards the stairs. "I can't tell you the number of times I lost control sliding down the banisters and bounced off that tree. Pappy always said I had an incredible talent for finding new and more interesting ways to injure myself."

With a soft chuckle, he pointed to the trunk. "You can still see the bloodstain from when I broke my nose."

I leaned in to take a closer look, but Grolfshin pulled me back with a giggle.

"I'm kidding." He pinched the bridge of his nose. "About the blood, not the nose."

"That must've hurt."

"Oh, it did. But then, I've always been a klutz."

"Really? Me too." I grinned. I'd never met anyone I had so much in common with.

"Most hominids are, my little cherub." Bringelkoopf spoke softly enough that Grolfshin couldn't hear him. But it's not as easy as you might think to have someone whisper in your ear and not say or do anything to give him away.

"Hmmm," Grolfshin said, "perhaps we share a family curse. Though I hope you aren't as bad as me. I was twenty-two before I made it through a whole year without breaking something."

"You're right. I'm not that bad. But I have bounced off the screen door twenty-seven different times. Mom says if I break thirty, she's gonna take it out of my allowance."

Grolfshin tweaked my nose. "Just try to keep this in one piece, hmm?"

I laughed. "Okay."

We stopped at a scene of a young boy and a majestic unicorn atop a breezy ocean bluff. The unicorn knelt so that the boy could reach up and touch his horn.

"This has always been my favorite," Grolfshin said.

I ran my fingers along the unicorn's feet and thought that it might be my favorite too.

"When I was a boy," he continued, "I used to spend hours trying to reach the unicorn's horn. I jumped, I bounced, I tried everything I could think of, but until my fifteenth birthday, the only way I could reach it was when Prantie hoisted me onto his shoulders."

His voice lifted as he mentioned my father. So did my heart.

"I'll never forget it. I'd spent two months camping in Vorkalis. I don't know if it was the fresh mountain air or the goat's milk, or what, but I grew two inches that summer. When I got home, the first thing I did was to try to reach the horn, and I did." He laughed. "But I was so surprised that when I turned to tell Prantie and Pappy, I slipped and fell."

Grolfshin chuckled when I stretched my hand up. My fingers were miles away.

"I think you've got a few years yet. Here, let me help." He lifted me up and when I slapped my hand on the horn, I felt closer to my father than ever.

Grolfshin tousled my hair, then set me down and waved Sammy over. "Come, let me show you around."

I'd always thought of castles like museums—cool places with lots of expensive, breakable things you couldn't touch. But this castle was filled with all sorts of orange, red and purple delights. And not a single breakable, non-touchable thing.

Yet the best part was how, in every single room, Grolfshin told me yet another story about him and my father, and how they'd gotten into no end of trouble together.

He made my father real to me, and I loved every minute of it.

The walls of the Grand Hall were lined with at least a hundred paintings of men with curly black hair and long skinny bodies.

"Dude, it's like your very own family photo album." Sammy thumped my shoulder, narrowly missing Bringelkoopf.

"Watch where you put those fingers, Buttercup," Bringelkoopf growled. Sammy couldn't hear him, but I scooted out of his arms' reach just in case.

Grolfshin gave me a few minutes to take it all in before he led me to the one I wanted most to see. My father must have been about my age at the time. He looked every bit the protective older brother Grolfshin had made him out to be.

Grolfshin smiled wistfully. "He was a good man, our father, King Talarcos Prios the Third. I remember when we had this one done. You see how Prantie's right arm is tucked behind Pappy? I fell out of a tree the day before and Prantie caught me. But his arm got crushed between me and a rock in the process, so he had to pose with his arm hidden."

It was exactly the family portrait I'd always longed to have. Except one with me in it.

"Pappy died seventeen years ago, and me and Prantie, well, we were never the same again. Pappy's death hit Prantie the hardest. It changed him, it really did."

Grolfshin looked down at me and tweaked my hair with a fond smile. "Jacob, it truly is good to see you, but tell me, how is your father?"

The question hit me like a jolt of electricity. "He died eight years ago," I whispered.

The blood drained from my uncle's face as he registered my words. "Oh God, Prantie, oh God." His body shook and I held him as tight as I could.

After a few minutes, he collected himself and pulled away.

"You look just like him, you know. You could be him when he was your age." The pain in his eyes matched the pain in his voice and I almost couldn't bear it.

And then, just like that, he seemed to recover. He tilted his head to the side and gave me a funny look. "Jacob, if your father died so long ago, may I ask how did you get here?"

At that moment, all I wanted was to tell him everything, so that he could tell me it was all going to be okay and we could live happily ever after. And if it hadn't been for Manservant, that's exactly what I would have done.

I'd just opened my mouth to blurt out all about the port when Manservant shuffled in and hovered near the statue of King Prios the First.

The castle's gray-haired butler was so huge that he barely fit through the doors. He didn't walk, he waddled. But he waddled so gracefully that it was easy to forget how huge he was.

"Your Majesty, if you please?"

"What?" Grolfshin scowled and stomped over to him.

I craned my big ears, but Manservant ducked his head and spoke too softly for me to hear. But I did catch a few angry snippets from Grolfshin.

"How long? When? Fine. I'll do it myself."

Grolfshin cast a furtive glance at me. "Jacob, something's come up. I need to step out for a moment. Wait for me here, okay?"

"Yeah, sure, Uncle," I said.

As soon as they were gone, I turned to Sammy. "Isn't this great? All these paintings? And that one of my dad?"

Sammy frowned. "I don't know, Jakey, there's something…wrong… about your uncle."

"What do you mean? What's wrong with him?"

"I can give you a list if you'd like," said Bringelkoopf.

Sammy scrunched his brows and tilted his head to the side. "I don't know exactly, but something feels fishy to me."

I couldn't believe it. My best friend was supposed to be happy for me.

"He said he saw you like eleven years ago, right?" Sammy asked.

"Yeah."

"And you know it's been at least eight years since he's seen your dad, right?"

"Yeah, so?"

"He was all 'Prantie' this and 'Prantie' that, yet we were here for like an hour before he asked about him. And he never asked how he died. Something about that doesn't seem right."

"Maybe he was just happy to see me."

"Or maybe he already knew the answer."

"Oh, come on. You saw how he reacted. There was no way he knew my dad was dead."

"Maybe not, but he's buttering you up for something, Jakey. And I don't like it."

"Buttercup is right. It would be his style, but don't tell him I said so," Bringelkoopf said.

Just then we heard the sound of rapidly approaching footsteps.

Sammy grabbed me by the shoulders. "Jakey, look, I know you wanna tell him, but give yourself a little more time, you know, to be sure, okay?"

I opened my mouth to protest but Sammy held up a hand to stop me.

"I'll do you a deal. If you still think I'm wrong tomorrow, tell him then, okay? Like I said before, if he's really a stand-up dude, he'll understand."

I just knew Sammy and Bringelkoopf were wrong about Grolfshin. But I had to admit that Sammy had never been wrong before, and I had only just met my uncle.

"Okay," I said grudgingly.

The door burst open and Grolfshin strode in, strung so tight he looked about to burst. He rubbed his hands together madly to keep them from twitching. It was a tactic I knew well.

"Jacob, I'm so sorry about that," he said.

"It's okay. Is everything alright?"

"Oh, yes, fine, fine, nothing to worry about. Dinner will be ready soon."

His voice was strained. He'd only been gone a few minutes, but it felt like everything had changed. I wanted to think it was just because I was uneasy after the conversation with Sammy, but I had a sinking feeling that wasn't it.

Grolfshin came over to admire the painting with me again. He swallowed, as if swallowing a deep pain. "Did you know your father was the King?"

"Really?" It wasn't as difficult to sound surprised as I'd thought it might be. After all, it's not every day you find out you're the heir to your father's throne.

"No way? Seriously?" Sammy asked.

"Yes," Grolfshin said, "he was just twenty-five when he became King. You know, your painting should be up there too, Jacob. You are, after all, the rightful heir to Portalia's throne."

I laughed. "Yeah, right, me a King? You're joking, right?"

"No, Jacob, I'm not joking. Your father never officially abdicated."

"Abdicated?"

"He never gave up his right to the throne. That means that you, as his only son, are the rightful King. Indeed, it is your duty by birth, and your destiny, Jacob, to be King of Portalia."

He studied me sadly for a moment, then scooped me into another bear hug and held me close. "Jacob, I cannot tell you how happy you've made me. I love you Jacob, I do."

And, just like when we'd first met, I clung to him. I had an uncle. And all I had to do was hold on tight and never let go. And push aside the nagging fear that something wasn't quite right.

I had thought that my dream of being an intergalactic musician would be the hardest to hold onto. But for that dream to come true, I'd only needed to step through a shimmering tree.

What I could not have known as I hugged my uncle, was that of all the dreams I'd ever had, the dream of an uncle who loved me was going to be the hardest dream of all to keep.

TO TRAP A MOUSE

GROLFSHIN HADN'T WARNED ME about the dinner guests. A woman and two men.

I frantically tweaked the tablecloth tassels, but my fingers wouldn't stop twitching.

Three pairs of strange eyes were riveted to me, watching my every move.

It didn't help that Sammy was well out of shin-kick range.

Grolfshin claimed mine was the seat of honor. It didn't feel that way to me.

I was all alone at the so called head of the table. Everyone else was clustered at the other end, where Grolfshin was headed. Sammy and the woman on one side, and the two men on the other.

As Grolfshin passed behind the woman, he brushed his fingers along her back and paused for a moment to allow his hand, and his gaze, to linger upon her.

Then he took his seat, directly across from me, and gestured to the man on his left. "Jacob, allow me to introduce Harold, Duke of Vorkalis."

Just looking at Harold made me shudder. He had a thick red beard and creepy yellow eyes that peered out from his shaggy mane. And when he curled his lips into what was probably meant to be a smile, he looked like a werewolf.

Grolfshin nodded to the man beside Harold. "Walthrin, Duke of Vorxal."

Walthrin was as disgusting as Harold was creepy. He was round and greasy and had likely not used his hands for anything more demanding than pulling apart chunks of food in his entire life. Soggy bread crumbs dribbled from his mouth when he nodded at me.

My stomach churned and goose bumps sprouted on my arms.

"And this," Grolfshin said, turning to the woman on his right, "is Beverly." His voice, like his face, lit up as he laced his fingers through hers.

Beverly wore a silky purple dress that complemented her long, radiant black hair perfectly. She made purple seem the most natural color for any woman to wear.

Her smile lit up the room and warmed away my Harold-and-Walthrin-induced shivers.

"Jacob," she said, her voice as warm and welcoming as her smile. "It's such a pleasure to meet you."

"Me too. I mean, you too," I said.

"I was very sorry to hear about your father. Please accept my condolences."

"Thank you." Only then did I realize that neither of the men had mentioned my father.

"And Sammy," Beverly continued, turning her wonderful smile to him. "Tell me, what do you think of Portalia?"

Sammy was taken by surprise. Nobody else had given any indication that they'd even seen him, let alone bothered to care if he had an opinion.

Sammy grinned. "Well, the food smells great!"

I couldn't have agreed more. As Manservant set the table with what looked like the most colorful thanksgiving feast I'd ever seen, the dining room exploded with sweet fruity smells.

"Oh, but it tastes even better, I assure you," Grolfshin said. "Dig in and see for yourself."

It might have been fun to watch the way everyone ate with their fingers, if it weren't for Walthrin and Harold.

But Harold and Walthrin were the only not-delightful things about the dining room.

There was a fireplace in every corner. Each one burned a different color flame and was surrounded by strictors in matching hues.

The wood walls were polished glossy smooth. They reflected the flickering from the fires, making it feel like we were sitting in the middle of a dazzling fireworks show.

But the most perfect thing about dinner was Manservant's almost magical ability to know what I wanted before I could ask for it.

He shuffled about, quietly and gracefully, and my plate and mug were never empty.

Despite my best efforts, though, there was no way I could sample everything. I looked forlornly at yet another dish I had not yet tried.

Grolfshin laughed. "Jacob, you act like this is your last meal."

"He probably wishes it could be," Bringelkoopf said.

I laughed and ignored the obnoxious not-a-ferret on my shoulder. Beverly laughed too. Her laugh was pleasant and friendly, and I liked it. It got me to thinking.

"Uncle Grolfshin, do you have any kids?"

Apparently, that was funny, because everybody laughed—well, everybody except Harold.

"No, Jacob, I'm not yet married." He smiled at Beverly. "But someday, perhaps."

"Can I ask another question?"

"By all means, Jacob, ask anything you want." He leaned forward and whispered loudly, "I have no secrets." Everybody laughed some more.

"Yeah, right," Bringelkoopf said.

"You told me about your father, but what about your mother?"

As soon as I asked it, I knew it was the wrong question. The room became completely silent. Beverly looked away, and Grolfshin fought to keep his smile on his face.

"My mother died when I was born, Jacob."

"Oh, I'm sorry."

"Of course, you couldn't have known. She was not very strong. Unfortunately, when she died, my father had a peasant woman nurse me. It was regrettable that he could not find a woman of good breeding to feed me. But life is not always fair."

"Ungrateful twit," Bringelkoopf muttered. "He always blames his weaknesses on that poor, sweet woman."

Grolfshin leaned back and regarded me with narrowed eyes. "Jacob, your birthday's in two days, isn't it?"

Something in his tone told me that the question he was really asking had nothing to do with my birthday.

"Yeah, it is."

He continued in an eerie voice. "Nephew, you never did tell me how you got here."

His smile lacked the loving-uncle goodness it had had earlier. The way he looked at me reminded me of a cat. And cats tend to eat mice.

My fingers sought out a fresh batch of tassels. "My dad left me a letter. In it, he told me about Portalia, and where to find the portal so I could come visit you."

"I see." Grolfshin brushed his fingers along his lips and studied me thoughtfully.

Harold's yellow eyes gleamed. "And you found the portal open?" His gravelly voice made my ears cringe. And his tone told me he did not believe me for one second.

"Yeah, I did."

Grolfshin raked his eyes over me. "Did your father say anything else in the letter?"

"Nope, that was it." A tassel gave way. I shoved it in my pocket and searched for another.

"Hmm, I see," Grolfshin said. "Tell me, Jacob, where did you get these clothes? One thing I remember about Earth is that the clothes, like the food, were so very bland."

Beverly squeezed his hand. "Sweetheart, the poor dear, you are bombarding him with questions. He's only just arrived."

My heart pounded in my throat. Michael had been right about the clothes. There was no denying that we would have stood out like sore thumbs in our jeans and sneakers.

But Michael had forgotten to suggest to us how we might explain that we were wearing Portalian clothes, rather than something from Earth.

"Oh strictor fever," Bringelkoopf hissed. I didn't know what that meant, though I had a sneaking suspicion it was not something generally said in polite company.

Fortunately the question didn't faze Sammy. He answered so quickly and smoothly that it even sounded true. Did I mention that Sammy was in drama club?

"Oh, these things? Jacob's dad had a chest full of Halloween costumes. At least, that's what we thought they were. Totally never thought they were clothes people actually wore."

I wasn't sure if Grolfshin bought Sammy's story. I was pretty certain that Harold did not, but I couldn't tell about Walthrin. He was too busy slobbering over his food.

Grolfshin leaned forward. He looked sad, as though he was about to tell me something unpleasant. "Jacob, there is something you should know. Portalia and Earth share not only a history but also a destiny. And we Prios men are the chosen guardians of that destiny. Your father was supposed to go to Earth and...."

Grolfshin paused and stared at his hands. "Jacob, your father was not a strong leader, but he knew this about himself. We knew that when it came time for us to finish what our forefathers started long ago, Portalia would need a strong leader. So we decided he would go to Earth and I would stay here."

Bringelkoopf hissed and dug his claws into my shoulder. I had to bite my tongue to keep from crying out at the pain.

"Then he married an Earthling." Grolfshin spat out "Earthling" as though we were an inferior species. Never mind that the Earthling in question was my mother.

"He should have married a woman of Guardian bloodlines, as Prios men have always done. But Prantos changed after Pappy died. And when he went to Earth, I knew then what I know now. He went there to escape. Jacob, I loved your father, but that doesn't change the fact that he abandoned his people and his kingdom. Abandoned us all."

Bringelkoopf was beside himself with fury. He embedded his claws so deeply in my shoulder that I was no longer sure they'd ever come out.

"But why didn't you ever go and talk to him?" I asked.

"Because I cannot open a port. I do not have the ability." He looked at me curiously. "I never knew your father had opened a permanent port. I never realized he had that much power."

All eyes were upon me as he spoke, except for Beverly's. She refused to look at me. And her face was creased with pain.

Grolfshin brightened. "But you are not like your father, Jacob. I can see it in your eyes. If you fulfill your duty, I believe we can continue our mission, our destiny."

Walthrin spoke up. "People will say he isn't really Prantos's son, or that Prantos is not dead at all."

Unfortunately, Walthrin's voice was just as slimy as the rest of him, and he clearly did not share Sammy's ability to politely talk around a mouthful of food.

"That may be," Grolfshin said, "but don't worry, Jacob. I have no doubt you are my beloved nephew, and, though it pains me so, I also have no doubt that my dear brother is dead."

"How will you prove who I am?" I asked.

"Dude," Sammy said, "you look just like him. Any moron could see that."

Walthrin snorted. "That won't be enough. You'll need more. Like the port."

"Hmm, you may be right." Grolfshin stroked his beard stubble. "Walthrin, have Vierkins, Plinkens, and Fowsters meet us here tomorrow after lunch."

My neck tingled, and not just from Bringelkoopf's claws.

Grolfshin turned to me. "Showing us the port will prove who you are. For only Prantos's son could know its location. I will insist the throne is yours, and I will declare that anyone who questions your right to the throne is a traitor."

He nodded, satisfied. "Don't worry, Jacob, I will be with you every step of the way."

Then he did something peculiar. He looked to Harold, as if seeking permission. When Harold nodded, Grolfshin rang his handy bell.

Seconds later, Manservant sailed in and set a leather bundle in front of Grolfshin.

Bringelkoopf stuck his nose out and hissed when he saw the bundle. "Jacob, be careful."

Grolfshin unfolded the leather gingerly. "Jacob, you may not have known this, but your father was quite a talented musician. Do you play?"

"I try." I barely heard myself speak. My eyes and thoughts were riveted to the wooden flute Grolfshin held up.

Although I'd never seen it before in my life, I desperately wanted to hold it.

As if reading my mind, Grolfshin brought the flute to me and placed it carefully in my hands.

My fingers forgot all about the tassels as I ran them across the glorious instrument. It was smooth and sleek and had a burnt cinnamon and metallic smell that stirred something within me.

A voice in my head told me that I should fling it far from me. But my soul had longed for this instrument and I felt an irresistible urge to play it. Although I had not yet grown into my ears, it never occurred to me that I couldn't.

I ignored the voice and lifted the instrument to my lips. Like a hungry mouse takes the cheese from the trap.

For a few blissful minutes, I lost myself in the sweet, sad music my soul chose to play. The accompanying sound that assaulted my ears was not nearly as wretched as the sound my violin usually makes. But I wouldn't have cared if it had been.

When the song finished, I reluctantly set the instrument down and opened my eyes.

An icy chill overcame me.

Harold's curled lips, furry face and yellow eyes made him look hauntingly like a wolf moving in for the kill. I'd have liked it better if he'd cringed and told me how awful I sounded.

And Grolfshin was staring at me with a hunger in his eyes. Hunger, yes, but also sadness and regret. Somehow I knew the sadness wasn't because of my lack of musical ability.

Sammy jumped up. "It's been a long day, Jakey. I don't know about you, but I'm beat."

"Yeah, me too," I said.

"Of course, of course, my boy," Grolfshin said. "How inconsiderate of me. You need your rest. Manservant will show you to your rooms."

Before we made it out of the room, Harold spoke to me one more time. "Jacob, tomorrow you will show us your father's port?"

I shuddered. It was not a request.

And I was surprised at how hard it was to rip my gaze from his.

* * *

My castle bedroom was bigger than my entire house back on Earth. It even had its own fireplace.

Bringelkoopf leapt from my shirt the moment Manservant shut the door. "Phew, it's about time. I can't believe all that nonsense Grolfshin said about your father."

I slumped on the bed and the oversized comforter almost swallowed me up. "I don't know. It's hard to know what to believe."

"What? Are you serious?"

I shrugged.

"You know, you are not so unlike your father, Jacob." Bringelkoopf's tone matched his droopy tail.

That was the problem. Apparently, my father had shared more than big ears, black tumbleweed hair, and a no-sun-needed-tan with me. Grolfshin said he'd gone to Earth to hide. I knew all about hiding. But I'd wanted to believe that my father had been stronger than me.

Sammy tiptoed in before Bringelkoopf could say anything else. "So, if it looks like a fish, flops like a fish and smells like a fish, what is it?"

"Huh?"

"Really?" Bringelkoopf said. "All that advanced technology and education on Earth, and they churn out brilliant humanoids who can say big words like 'huh'?"

"A fish," Sammy said. "You call it a fish. As in, your uncle is a fish. You didn't buy all that nonsense Grolfshin said about your father, did you?"

"Apparently he did," said Bringelkoopf.

"What would you know about my father?" I snapped at Sammy.

I regretted the words as soon as they came out. The truth was, Sammy knew as much about my father as I did. He was the only one I'd ever been able to talk to about wanting to connect with my father through music and the stars.

"Sammy, I'm—"

"No." His lips quivered and tears streamed down his face. "Jakey, I know you want Grolfshin to be the father you think you never had. But you had a father. My father took one look at me the minute I was born and walked out. Your father didn't leave you, Jakey. He died. It sucks that he's gone, but you can't replace him with his brother."

"I know. But he's my uncle and he says he loves me."

"Dude, just because someone *says* something doesn't make it true. You know that."

"You said he'd think I was a threat, but he practically told me I had to take the throne."

"Seriously? 'I will defend your right to the throne, but first show us the port?' The port, which, by the way, was the most important thing Michael suggested you not tell this guy. Are you really not seeing this?"

"Guess not," Bringelkoopf said "Of course, that is a very common flaw with bipeds."

"Jakey," Sammy said, "you're a good guy, you see the best in everyone, and I like that about you. But promise me you won't show Grolfie and his creepy pals the portal, okay?"

"But what am I supposed to do? He's going to ask me to show him tomorrow."

Sammy shrugged. "Take him on a wild goose chase, and say 'Sorry, can't find it.'"

"Yeah, because he totally won't suspect anything," Bringelkoopf said.

"So, you got a better idea?"

"Not yet. I'm thinking," Bringelkoopf admitted.

Sammy yawned. "Well, how 'bout we all think while we sleep?"

"First sensible thing you've said." Bringelkoopf slid under my pillow and promptly fell asleep.

Shortly after Sammy left, Grolfshin came in. He sat beside me and tried to brush my curly hair behind my ears. I didn't have the heart to tell him it was pointless. Besides, he had the exact same hair, so he probably already knew.

"I am so glad you are here, Jacob."

"Me too." I only wished I meant it as much as I would have before dinner.

A strange look of sorrow flashed across his face. He gave up on my hair and contented himself with tucking the comforter around me instead.

"I love you, Jacob, I really do."

The way he said it made it sound like an apology.

He kissed me goodnight and left and I fell asleep with a confused heart and dreamed the same terrifying dream all night long. It was a dream about a black wolf with yellow eyes and red fur. He loomed over a cowering purple puppy and snarled, speaking with Harold's voice. "If you can't get him to show you where the port is, we will."

* * *

I was only two bites into an exquisite Portalian breakfast feast when Grolfshin started in. "Jacob, Harold and the other dukes will be here this afternoon so that you can show us the port."

A cold knot grew in my stomach. "Yeah, this afternoon."

Except that wasn't going to happen, because Sammy had come up with a plan.

I cleared my throat. "So, after breakfast, Sammy and I were thinking about taking a look around. Is that alright with you, Uncle?"

Grolfshin laughed. "You don't need my permission, Jacob. You are the King, after all."

"And he has no intention of letting you go without a guard," whispered Bringelkoopf.

As if on cue, Grolfshin rang his bell. "I'll arrange one of my men... I mean, one of *your* men, to guide you."

"Oh, don't worry about it, we'll be fine," Sammy said. He pushed back from the table and tousled my hair. "Well, I'm stuffed, couldn't eat another bite. What about you?"

Sammy wasn't really stuffed. Getting up from a table with tasty food remaining was simply something Sammy didn't do. But it was part of the plan.

"Yeah, me too." I got up without looking at Grolfshin. "Well, see you later."

"Yeah," Sammy added. "We'll be back for lunch."

We wouldn't be, though. We intended to "get lost" and miss lunch altogether. Sammy had shoved his pockets full of food so we wouldn't starve.

It would be dinner time by the time we managed to find our way back. Too late to go to the port. At least, that was the plan.

Looking at Grolfshin, I started to feel guilty for deceiving him. Before I could change my mind, I dashed off with Sammy.

Grolfshin hollered after me, "Jacob, wait. Jacob. Be careful. Don't get lost."

"We won't," Sammy called back.

We darted out the front door and ran as fast as we could.

Just before we passed through the castle gates, I stopped to look back.

Grolfshin was standing at the top of the steps watching us.

I felt a twinge of remorse and waved at him.

He waved back. But something about the way he waved didn't comfort me.

Even across the distance, he looked like a hungry cat watching a seemingly unsuspecting mouse grab the cheese and sidestep the cleverly laid trap.

DISCOVERY

SAMMY AND I ran for at least an hour. We didn't stop until we reached a river and needed to decide which way to go.

Bringelkoopf heaved a sigh of relief. He crawled out from under my shirt flap and coiled up around my neck to soak in the heat from the sun.

"Wish you'd warned me I'd be getting tossed about like a strictor," he grumbled.

"So, where to now?" I asked him, figuring he knew the planet and we didn't.

Sammy was one step ahead of me. He pointed downriver. "Look."

Roland Harkins and a group of boys were leaping into the river from the overreaching limbs of an enormous tree. Roland was poised at the tip of the highest and flimsiest branch.

"Hey Roland!" Sammy called out.

Roland grinned in recognition and waved. Then he took a giant leap and plunged into the water with a mighty splash.

"Now, that's what I'm talking about," Sammy said, grinning from ear to ear.

Nothing about what I'd just seen appealed to me. I was terrified of water and of heights.

But I was beat from all the running. Not to mention the hike Bringelkoopf had taken us on last night. I could use a break.

"Go ahead," I said.

"Really? You sure?"

No, not really. "Yeah, just, you know, don't break anything."

"I won't." Sammy thumped my shoulder and dashed off.

I found a shady tree safely removed from the danger of water and leaned back to enjoy the show.

Roland scurried fearlessly up the tree. Even though he was the smallest, his splashes were the biggest. He and Sammy competed to see who had the goofiest back flip. Amazingly, Roland looked like he just might win.

As I watched them laughing and splashing, I couldn't shake the feeling that I was missing something important about Grolfshin and Harold.

Absorbed in my thoughts, I didn't register the rustling of the branches above me until something landed beside me with a soft thunk.

I turned with a start. And froze on the spot.

A boy had just hopped down from the frighteningly tall tree. He was about my age, and a few inches taller than me.

After casually brushing off a few stray leaves, he looked at me.

An electric tingle coursed through me.

He had the brightest, most radiant smile ever. Like the smile in my dreams. Only better.

"Hi, I'm Milokah," he said.

His voice was a balm of happiness to my ears. And Milokah was the most perfect name I'd ever heard. I wanted to roll it off my tongue, but I was too spellbound to speak.

My fingers longed for paper and pen so they could glide his name onto the page.

And my ears desperately wanted to hear the vibrations of his voice again.

Milokah stood and watched me expectantly.

I realized it was my turn to speak.

"Jacob." It was my most mouse-like squeak ever. I didn't trust myself to try anything more complex. Like "Hello."

Fortunately, it was enough. He grinned even more brightly, though I wouldn't have dreamt it possible, and sat down beside me. Right beside me.

He had a bright yellow fruit in his hand. There were two bites missing. He held it out. "Apple?"

It looked scrumptious. But I could hardly breathe, let alone speak. He was so close that his breath tickled my cheek. And when he shifted to get more comfortable, his foot fell on top of my ankle.

Sammy had told me about stuff like this. Of course he was talking about girls. Not boys.

I never thought I'd actually meet a boy who would make my heart do all the funny things it was suddenly doing. Things it had never done before.

His hair was wavy, thick, and jet-black. It matched his dark olive green eyes perfectly.

His skin was darker than mine, but not as dark as my father's. He probably spent lots of time in the sun. The sun looked good on him. Yes, the sun suited him nicely.

When I made no move to accept the apple, he shrugged and took a bite. It sounded delightfully crisp.

He captivated me in a way nobody ever had. And—I was certain—nobody else ever could. My face turned a shade redder every time he glanced at me. Which he did between every bite.

He sat and munched, oblivious that he had just turned my entire world upside down.

To my brain, he looked no more or less special than any other boy. But to my heart, he was the most beautiful person in the world.

When he finished his apple he chucked the core into the river and turned to watch me watching him again.

I didn't realize how big and goofy the grin was on my face was until he laughed and threw a leaf at me.

I giggled and threw one back.

After a few more leaves, his laughter subsided. He sat quietly and stared into my eyes. And I did the same.

That's when I figured it out. His eyes. They were more dazzling than stars in the night sky. They didn't sparkle like Michael's. They did something far more spectacular—they gazed into my soul and spoke to me.

I felt like a man long stranded in the desert who has just stumbled upon an oasis.

And that's when the strangest thing happened. I felt myself begin to grow into my ears.

I didn't know what falling in love had to do with me growing into my ears. But it didn't really matter. Sitting with Milokah, I'd never felt more right.

"I think somebody's in love," crooned a soft voice in my ear. I'd forgotten about the not-a-ferret on my shoulder. By the tone of his chuckle, I think he knew what was happening. I laughed and scratched him behind the ears, probably not the reaction he was expecting.

"Can I pet him?" Milokah asked.

"Sure."

Milokah giggled softly and brushed his fingers gently through Bringelkoopf's wiry fur. He thought Bringelkoopf was cute and adorable, and wasn't I lucky to have him.

"What does he eat?"

A surge of mischief came over me. "Scraps, stuff you would usually throw away. I have to be careful, or he'll get into the garbage."

"Does he do tricks?"

Bringelkoopf dug his claws into me as a warning, but I couldn't resist. Besides, he was supposed to help me. With his help, I had just successfully uttered a complete sentence.

"Sure he does." I set him on the ground. "Bringie, lie down."

With a threatening glare, Bringelkoopf plunked down.

Milokah clapped his hands and giggled with delight.

"Roll over."

Bringelkoopf twisted to his other side. His eyes blazed with the promise of payback.

Not certain how far I could push him, I picked him up and returned him to his familiar place on my shoulder.

I heard an angry growl. It didn't seem worth the risk to reach up with my vulnerable fingers and scratch his chin.

Milokah leapt up and held out his hand. "Come with me?"

I looked over to where Sammy and Roland had been. They weren't there. But I could still hear voices and splashing in the distance. They must have moved to a better tree.

My fingers tingled as I put my hand in his.

He pulled me up and when I got to my feet, he didn't let go.

Milokah and I were alone. And he was holding my hand. I felt giddy.

He hauled me off to a grassy meadow, where we waded through orange-and purple-bristled grass. The bristles looked sharp and pointy, but I followed him dreamily anyway. He could have led me happily right off a cliff.

We sat down together at a warm and sunny spot.

He pulled two stalks up by their roots. He handed the purple one to me and kept the orange one.

"Do what I do," he said.

He plucked the bristles, careful not to squash them, and collected them in the bottom of his shirt. It took me a few minutes to get the hang of it. They were soft and feather-like and bruised easily.

Once we had our bristles, we cupped them carefully in our hands and stood up.

Milokah blushed. It was the first time I'd seen him look nervous. He gestured to the sky. "Together. Ready?"

I nodded.

We tossed the bristles as high as we could. I expected them to start fluttering back down. Instead, they hovered and mingled together.

Milokah took my hand and threaded his fingers with mine. "Dance?"

I was too entranced to move. The bristles' many-faceted edges reflected the bright sunlight like mirror balls. Bursts of purple and orange glittered off Milokah's dark skin and jet-black hair. He looked stunning.

"Dance?" His voice wavered, as if he feared I might say no.

"Yes." I followed his lead.

The bristles fluttered ever so slowly downwards.

For several long and blissful minutes, I was lost to another world, one where only he and I, and our beautiful soul music, existed.

We swished and swayed beneath the softly floating purple and orange bristles. My soul quivered, purring within me, as if Milokah were plucking its strings.

Our souls were dancing to the same music. I know, because I heard it and the look on Milokah's face told me he heard it too.

The music finished just as the last bristle floated to the ground.

We lay on our backs with our arms behind our heads and our elbows touching, gazing up at the sky, soaking up the sun, and snacking on blades of grass. Every single one was sweet and chewy, yet no two ever tasted the same. Not quite like gummy bears, but pretty close.

"I like to lie out at night sometimes, just to watch the stars," Milokah said.

"Me too. When I look at the stars, I see beauty and music and I dream big dreams. Because, if you can't see beauty and dream big, what's the point?"

"I know what you mean." And I knew that he did. He really did.

After slurping down the juice from a particularly tasty blade of grass, I used the hem of my shirt to wipe my mouth. When I did, Milokah looked over and frowned.

He hiked my shirt up to get a better look at my scraped side.

"What's that?" He asked.

"Oh, it's nothing. Only a little scratch, really."

"What happened?"

"Um, I sort of fell into something."

He gave me a funny look. Even though he couldn't have known better, he looked very much like my mom had when I told her the same thing. Like he knew there was more to the story. Fortunately, like my mom, he didn't pry.

"My sister makes salves. I can ask her to make one and bring it for you, if you'd like."

The scrapes really weren't that big a deal. But all I could think of was how much I wanted to see him again. "Yeah," I said. "I'd like that."

We fell into a suddenly awkward silence then.

Milokah tweaked a few blades of grass and glanced sideways at me a few times. He had a knowing glint in his eye, as if he knew a secret of mine.

I started frantically going back over the things I'd said. I'd said lots of dorky things, but I couldn't think of any big secrets I'd let slip. I hadn't mentioned Michael or anything.

"What?" I asked him, when I could stand it no more.

He shrugged, nonchalantly, then ducked his head shyly. "So, you're from Earth?"

His words floored me. Michael had said that most Portalians didn't know about Earth. I'd figured it was something kids wouldn't know, and only a few select adults.

"How'd you know?"

He grinned. "I saw you come through the portal."

I remembered the sound of something crashing through the forest. "That was you?"

He nodded.

"How did you know about the Portal?"

"My father and uncle are Portalkeepers. Didn't your father tell you about us?"

"No. He died when I was four." I swallowed a sudden lump. No matter how many times I said it, it never seemed to be any less painful.

Milokah cried out, horrified. "King Prantos is *dead*?" He looked at me intently, desperately hoping he'd misheard. When I said nothing, he looked away.

"I'm sorry. I'm so sorry." His voice held more anguish than even Grolfshin's.

It dawned on me, then. He knew who I was. My mind was spinning with everything that had happened, everything I'd learned, since Sammy and I stepped through the tree in my clubhouse.

I had so many questions. And suddenly, I realized, maybe Michael and Grolfshin weren't the only ones I could ask.

Milokah beat me to it.

"How much do you know about what's happened? Since your father left?"

"Hardly anything." Then, without thinking, I blurted, "Tell me, please. Tell me what you know."

And he did.

After his son was born, the King, my father, started disappearing every year. He returned only during Portal Week.

Grolfshin ruled in the King's absence, and life went on. Portalians loved and laughed and enjoyed life, as they had done for thousands of years.

Then, eight years ago, the King did not return as he was supposed to. For years, the Portalkeepers waited dutifully. With each year, their confidence wavered. Two years ago, they stopped waiting altogether.

"Then why were you there?" I interrupted.

"Because I had faith in King Prantos. I knew he would not abandon us."

"Nice boy, for a human. I like him," Bringelkoopf said.

"And they let you wait there, all by yourself? At night?"

He grinned. "They don't know that I know where the portal is."

Bringelkoopf chuckled. "Very nice boy. Very nice indeed."

"Don't worry, Jacob, the Cats sleep during Portal Week. It's not like it's dangerous."

Bringelkoopf's teeth rattled when Milokah mentioned the Cats. I, on the other hand, was blissfully ignorant about the Talarkin hill beasts, which Bringelkoopf later told me were huge, koopf-and-human-hating monsters with razor blades for teeth and butcher knives for claws.

Milokah continued. Two years after my father disappeared, taking me, his only known heir, with him, Grolfshin declared himself King. His first act was establishing a school for musically gifted youth.

At first, parents considered it a great honor when their kids were invited to attend. But they soon realized their children weren't allowed to come home, and promises of school visitations never seemed to materialize.

Before long, parents stopped bringing their children in to be evaluated. That's when things started getting bad. Grolfshin decreed that *all* children must submit to testing. Parents of those who didn't would be imprisoned. He also demanded the best of all crops and animals as payment rightfully due the King.

"Why does he want the kids in his school so badly?" I asked. "And why does he need the crops and animals? The castle farmlands are huge."

"Nobody knows. They say he has enough to feed every person on Portalia for a year."

"Or an army," Bringelkoopf said.

That niggling feeling that I was missing something important popped up again.

"Two years ago, people began disappearing," Milokah said, "and I've heard stories of horrible screams coming from the castle dungeons. My father thinks that Grolfshin is being controlled by the Duke of Vorkalis."

My skin crawled at the mention of the Duke of Vorkalis. Harold.

I remembered the dream of the wolf and the cowering purple puppy. And I felt my dream of an uncle who loved me slip away, like sand through fingers.

Milokah continued. "My dad grew up with your dad and uncle. He says he can't believe the Grolfshin he knew would do the things he does. But he said Grolfshin's always been weak, and without his brother around, he would be easy to manipulate."

"You sound as though you feel sorry for him."

"Some people take their pain and turn it into love, and some into hate. It's easier to hate than to love. Grolfshin believed he was abandoned by the one person he loved. I think Harold took advantage of that. It's not that I don't blame him for the things he does, Jacob, it's just that I also feel sorry for him."

That's when Milokah dropped his bombshell. He peered into the depths of my very soul as he spoke. "Portalians have lost hope. But not me. You give me hope, Jacob Prios. I have faith in you. I know you will be a great King."

His words terrified me. It did not help that Bringelkoopf did not chortle, or chuckle, or snicker, but merely rubbed his head against my ear and purred.

Milokah reached up and scratched my spoiled rotten not-a-ferret. "I know you can talk, Bringelkoopf."

"Then why," asked Bringelkoopf indignantly, "did you ask if I could do tricks?"

He giggled. "I just wanted to see if you would."

Bringelkoopf snorted, but he leaned into Milokah's fingers. "A little further down, that's it, ah, yes, just the spot."

Just then I heard Sammy calling my name. "Jacob!"

He was headed right towards us.

A funny look crossed his face when he saw me with Milokah.

I jumped up as if I'd been stung.

Milokah got up too. He smiled and moved towards me to close the massive gap I'd just created between us.

But as soon as he did, I stepped away and his smile faltered.

He looked at Sammy, and by the time his eyes came back around to me, I saw comprehension. And a pain that stabbed at my heart.

He looked like I'd just gutted him. I couldn't bear it and looked away.

As Sammy got closer, he scrunched his brows tighter and tighter together as he looked back and forth between Milokah and me.

I panicked. "I gotta go."

"Okay." Milokah choked on his words. "See you later?" He tried to look into my eyes but I ducked to avoid his gaze.

"I don't know," I mumbled. I started jogging towards Sammy before the words were all the way out.

"Remember what I said," Milokah called after me.

He sounded so sad. And I hated myself. I picked up my pace.

Just before I reached Sammy, I turned to look back. But he was already gone.

"Who was that kid?" Sammy asked.

"Nobody, just some kid. The grass tastes like gummy bears. You should try it."

Sammy frowned and looked like he was about to say something. Instead, he shook his head and started walking.

My heart lurched. My guts twisted into a ball. And the memory of every time I'd ever insisted I wasn't gay came back to me. Those lies had always tasted bitter. But not even all of them combined had seared my tongue with as much agony as the words I'd just spoken.

Nobody. Just some kid.

Milokah wasn't nobody. Our souls had danced together. Yet I'd denied him to protect my secret. And for what? In two days, Sammy would know. Yet for those two days, I'd taken the gift of Milokah's soul and cast it aside like a piece of trash.

My ears felt bigger than they ever had. Like ears I could never hope to grow into. And I felt a huge void in my soul. I wasn't sure I'd ever hear its music again.

"What'd he mean, that kid, when he said, 'remember what I said'?"

I told Sammy everything Milokah had told me. Except for the part where he said he had faith in me, and that I gave him hope.

Sammy suggested we return to Michael's immediately. I knew that was the smart thing to do. Even so, I kept hoping for a miracle that would make everyone else wrong, and prove that Grolfshin really was the loving uncle I so desperately wanted him to be.

Bringelkoopf sensed my hesitation. "Or did you miss the part about the dungeons and the horrible screaming?"

He was right. They were both right. I just couldn't bring myself to say it.

Bringelkoopf and Sammy let me set the pace. I started slowly. But the more I thought, the faster I walked, and the angrier I became.

I was angry with Grolfshin for not being the uncle I wanted him to be.

I was angry with my father for dying when I was so young.

I was angry with Michael for not telling me about Grolfshin, and for allowing me to hope in an uncle he knew I couldn't have. How could I love my uncle, knowing what he was doing?

I was angry with Milokah for making me fall in love with him. And for having faith in me and telling me that I would be a great King.

Milokah was wrong about me. I was the mouse that hid. I was the boy who denied his own truth. He'd seen the way I reacted when Sammy saw us together. How could he hope in me?

Then it hit me. The person I was angriest with was...me. Because I was not the person Milokah thought I was. And I could not be the person I needed to be.

Suddenly I heard a voice from deep within me, a voice I'd only ever heard in my dreams: "You *are* that person, my son. You have to be. These are *your* people. This is *your* destiny."

I felt like screaming. And I was about to, when Sammy clamped his hand over my mouth and dragged me behind a nearby bush.

That's when I heard them. Horses. The voices of men. And Grolfshin.

"We have to find them before tomorrow," said one of the men. "If we don't, Harold will be most displeased, and that would not—"

"Don't you think I know that, you imbecile? How was I supposed to know my brother's little mongrel runt and his obnoxious friend would take off like that?"

The horses plodded towards us, clip-clop, clip-clop, one hoof in front of another.

"But we will find him." Grolfshin sounded like he was trying to convince himself more than anyone. "And he will give us what we want. I know he will."

He was so close that I could smell the sweat from his horse and hear the scratching of his beard stubble against his leather gloves as he rubbed his chin.

Sammy closed his eyes tight. It seemed like such a good idea that I did the same.

Grolfshin and his men rode by with agonizing slowness.

With every clip-clop, I heard my uncle's words. Over and over again. Mocking my love. Mocking my hope.

My brother's little mongrel runt.

I'd loved Grolfshin. I'd wanted to believe he loved me too.

The pain was excruciating. I just wanted it to be over. I just wanted to go home.

When the last horse had passed by, I opened my eyes. Bringelkoopf slid down from my shoulder and slithered off into the bushes. I wondered briefly where he was going.

Then I saw Sammy. He was staring over my shoulder, his eyes open wide with fright, and his face drained of all color.

I didn't need to look behind me to know that Grolfshin had found us.

IMPRISONED

WE WERE SURROUNDED by men with dogs. Not cuddly little lapdogs who could be bribed with a belly scratch, but snarling, foaming-at-the-mouth hounds.

I had a horrible sinking feeling in my gut. The feeling you get when you know something to be unquestionably true.

This was not a situation that Sammy could bail us out of with his clever wit or a charming grin. And our only ally had just turned tail, literally, and beaten a safe retreat.

Grolfshin rode up on a huge black horse and towered over me.

"Hello, nephew. Are you lost? You're heading the wrong way." His smile oozed sweetness, but his eyes were dark.

Grolfshin's horse was frighteningly close. When I tried to back away, he snorted, spraying my face with a warm stickiness that made his master chuckle.

"Should we tie 'em up?" asked a man who, I couldn't help but notice, bore an eerily strong resemblance to his snarling companion. The dog strained at his leash, looking like he wanted nothing more in this world than to take a big bite of Jacob. The man clearly hoped I'd give him an excuse to give his dog what he wanted.

A flash of remorse crossed Grolfshin's face, but it was gone as quickly as it had come. "Of course, you twit. What do you think?"

The man bound our hands tightly behind us, then flung us effortlessly onto two huge, scary horses and tied our ropes to the saddles. At least we weren't going to die falling off.

I wondered what was happening tomorrow, making Grolfshin so desperate to get us back by then. Then I remembered. Tomorrow was my birthday. Maybe he was worried I'd miss my surprise party. I suspected his definition of a surprise party was very different from mine.

My thoughts began to wander as we plodded toward whatever my loving uncle had in store for me. As far as I knew, I'd never ridden a horse before. But the rocking motion, the clip-clop of hooves, and the creak of the saddle all seemed strangely familiar to me.

And suddenly, the combined smell of horse sweat and leather flooded me with a crisp, crystal-clear memory of my father. And Grolfshin.

It was the first memory I'd ever had of Grolfshin and of Portalia.

* * *

Rocco, Little Me's big black-and-brown canine ball-retrieval maniac, leapt up and down, begging his boy to throw the ball. Which Little Me happily did, over and over. But along the way, he and Rocco had lost sight of the horses, and Daddie and Uncie.

That was a no-no, so they worked their way back to Little Me's favorite yellow tree, the one with the extra plump and tasty orange leaves. When they got there, Little Me did not like what he saw. Daddie and Uncie were arguing.

"You would sell out all of humanity for your new master?" yelled Daddie. "Don't you find it the least bit upsetting that he was the last person seen with Father before he died?"

"You aren't seriously accusing the Duke of Vorkalis of Father's death?"

"Father never fell off a horse in his life. Yet Harold would have us believe he was thrown from his horse because of a...rabbit? And you would show him the port to Earth? Can't you see that they are using you?"

"At least they are trying to help. You live a life of luxury on Earth with your Earthling wife, yet you share none of it with us. What are you *waiting* for?"

"This is not about what Earth can do for us. This is about fulfilling our destiny. And brother, I tell you, I begin to think they are not from Portalia at all. I do not believe they care for humans, be they Earthlings or Portalians."

"Of course they are from Portalia. From where else would they be?"

The yelling stopped, and Little Me thought the fight was over. But when Daddie looked over at Little Me he looked very, very sad and when he spoke, Little Me could tell he was crying.

"Brother, I am sorry. It is more than I should have asked of you. I will take my son home, and then I shall return."

"Take your son home?"

"Laney does not like it here. Give me two days. Promise me you will tell them nothing."

Something happened then. Little Me couldn't quite see it, but suddenly Daddie let out a howl that rivaled any of Rocco's. "You already told them? How could you? Nooooooo!"

Daddie ran to Little Me, swept him up and leapt onto his horse. He spun toward Grolfshin. "I must go close it. I will return in two days. Brother, I hope I am not too late."

With that they were off, Rocco bounding beside them, his tongue flapping in the wind. Little Me waved his chubby hand at Uncie and said, "Bye-bye Uncie." But they were too far away for Uncie to hear him. Then he snuggled up in his father's arms, lulled by the rocking motion of the horse, the creak of saddle leather, and the smell of horse sweat.

* * *

My horse stumbled, jolting me back to the present. I was still on a horse, but secured by a rope, not the strong, comforting arms of my father.

If I'd needed more than merely being bound and tied to a horse to convince me that Grolfshin was lying, that memory had done it. Grolfshin had said he hadn't seen me since I was one, but the Little Me in my memory was old enough to run and throw a ball. I was pretty sure one-year-olds didn't do that.

And my father hadn't gone to Earth to hide, like Grolfshin claimed. He'd planned to return. And he hadn't wanted Grolfshin to show Harold the port. But in the memory, Grolfshin had known where the port was. If so, why did he need me?

What I would not have given, at that moment, for something furry to dig its claws into my shoulders and whisper a sarcastic insult into my ear.

* * *

I quickly realized that every book I'd ever read that included a castle failed to properly describe a dungeon.

Yes, the dungeon in my castle was dimly lit with flickering torches on the walls. Yes, the cells were dark, the light from the torches never quite making it beyond the bars. And yes, it was a terrifying place.

But what the books had left out was the oh-so-important part about the smell. Obviously, a dungeon was not a place anybody deemed worthy of cleaning. If my lungs would have let me, I would have stopped breathing altogether to avoid the putrid smell. Unfortunately, my lungs refused to cooperate.

The guard threw Sammy in one cell and me in another. He grinned as he clanked the grates shut. When he left, taking his lantern with him, I no longer cared about the stench.

I was alone, in a dark dungeon, without my lifelong protector and best friend. It was just like being in sixth grade, only much much worse. I choked on a laugh. I'd officially found something that sucked even more than Archer Middle School. If only that were funny.

It seemed like many hours, but had probably only been a few minutes, when the darkness was punctuated by the sound of footsteps and the glow of an approaching lantern.

I tensed and waited as the footsteps came to a halt in front of my cell.

Grolfshin propped himself against the bars and inspected his fingers. "Jacob." He paused to pull a strand of hair from his robe. "Jacob, Jacob."

After all that had happened, a part of me still hoped he would fling open the grate, grab me up, and tell me he was sorry. But even I knew that wasn't going to happen.

"Why are you doing this?" I asked.

Like before, I thought I saw a brief flicker of sadness and remorse cross his face. His hands flapped almost as if he was fighting an inner battle.

Yet, whatever inner torment I thought I might have seen on his face, his voice held no sign of it. I began to wonder if I'd seen anything at all.

"Your father wasn't talented enough to open a permanent port, Jacob. You know what I think?" He strummed the bars of the cell like strings on a guitar. "I think *you* opened a port. Tell me, dear nephew, did you think to close it behind you?"

Grolfshin grinned victoriously at the look of horror on my face. "Jacob," he said with eerie calmness, "tell me where the port is. I need to know."

I mustered every ounce of courage I had. It wasn't much, but it was enough to raise my voice above a terrified squeak. "I trusted you, I loved you. And you said you loved me."

This time I was sure of what I saw. I'd caught him off guard, and glimpsed an inner battle before he regained control of himself. It came and went in less than a second, but it was there.

"It doesn't have to be this way, Jacob. We can still work together."

At the scuffle of more footsteps descending the dungeon steps, he gestured into the shadows. "Maybe *this* will help jog your memory."

I trembled, expecting to meet a dungeon master intent on torturing the truth out of me. It wouldn't take long.

But it was no dungeon master. There was to be no torture. It was something far, far worse than that.

The man who'd resembled his dog loomed into view with a malicious grin plastered across his face. And a rope in his hand. Cackling like a hyena, he tugged viciously on the rope.

Milokah and a woman, a very pregnant woman, stumbled forward.

My heart caught in my throat. I leapt up angrily and Grolfshin laughed in delight.

The guard appeared equally pleased with my reaction. He cackled even more loudly as he dragged Milokah and the pregnant woman past my cell.

"Jacob," Milokah cried out, "don't tell him anything."

The man silenced him with a slap across the face.

"No!" I flung myself at Grolfshin, oblivious to the bars between us. I don't know who was more surprised, me or Grolfshin.

Seeing Milokah in danger, a switch inside me flipped. Suddenly, I was not scared, worried, or nervous. No, I was furious. Livid. It was like nothing I had ever experienced.

"Don't you dare." I slammed my fists against the bars of the cell.

Grolfshin's smirk was short-lived as heavy footsteps scurried down the stairs and Manservant's urgent voice called out, "Your Majesty!"

Grolfshin spun with a snarl. "I'm busy."

"Yes, Your Majesty. Harold, Duke of Vorkalis—"

"Yes, Manservant, I know who Harold is."

"He's here, Your Majesty. He'd like a word with you."

Grolfshin's anger was abruptly replaced with fear. "Tell him I'll be up momentarily."

"Yes, Your Majesty." Manservant disappeared back up the steps. Grolfshin pinned my hands against the bars. "You listen to me, nephew. I will be back in thirty minutes, and you will give me what I want."

"Never."

Grolfshin lowered his voice and pulled me close. "Jacob, you will either tell me, or you will tell Harold." He shuddered. "But one way or the other you will tell us." He choked on what sounded like a sob. "You said you trusted me, you loved me?"

Moisture welled up in his eyes. "Then trust me now. Please."

I thought about the dream I'd had of the wolf and the cowering purple puppy. I couldn't help myself. I felt sorry for him.

He turned to leave. "In case you're thinking of opening a port, you should know that you're one hundred feet below ground. There are no ports from here. There is nowhere to go."

With that he strode briskly away. I watched the light of his lantern fade until there was nothing left but darkness. But in my mind, all I saw was a cowering purple puppy.

"Jacob?" It was Sammy.

"Sammy, are you okay?" I whispered as loudly as I dared.

"Yeah, I'm okay. But Jacob, what're we going to do?"

"Don't worry. I'll think of something." I sounded more confident than I felt.

I was scared. Scared for me. Scared for Sammy. But my gut twisted with in an entirely different kind of fear and agony at the thought of Milokah being hurt.

"Milokah," I called into the darkness. "Are you guys alright?" Cold fingers constricted my heart as I waited to hear his answer.

His reply was faint. "Jacob you've got to get us out of here. Telly's going to have her baby. It can't be born in here. Jacob, please. Do something."

Milokah sounded like he had a pretty good idea of what was going to happen to us, and the baby, if we didn't escape. But I had absolutely no idea how to get us out, other than by telling Grolfshin what he wanted. Which was starting to sound very tempting.

Then I heard the sweetest sound in all the universe—the sarcastic voice of my not-a-ferret friend. "Well, if you keep walking like that, eventually you'll wear a hole in the ground, maybe even deep enough to be your own grave."

"Bringelkoopf! I thought you'd left me."

"You thought I'd left you?"

"I'm sorry. I should have known better."

"Yes, you should have." He made no effort to hide his wounded feelings. "You think I enjoyed slinking down through the sewers like a common rat?"

Bringelkoopf had only left me to avoid capture. How could I have doubted him? But I didn't have time to worry about the hurt feelings of my not-a-ferret friend. "Look, you may not want to stay. They'll be back soon, and I have no idea how to get out."

"Well, why do you think I'm here?"

My heart leapt. "Do you know where the keys are? Can you get them?"

"No, I cannot get the keys. What am I, a pet monkey?"

"Then how are you going to get us out of here?"

"I'm not. Jacob, only you can get us out of here."

The relief and hope that Bringelkoopf's appearance had generated vanished instantly.

"Me? What am I supposed to do? *Wish* us out of here?"

"Hm, not a bad idea, I suppose—that is, if you were a fairy."

"Please don't make jokes, Bringelkoopf. This is serious."

"Yes, I know it's serious, and sitting here moping isn't gonna get you, Buttercup, or your boyfriend and his sister out of this."

"But what am I supposed to do?"

"Just a thought, but have you considered opening a port?"

I shook my head. "No, we're like a hundred feet below ground, and that won't do us any good. Besides, Grolfshin said there probably wasn't a port here anyway."

"That's true for opening a port to Earth. But Earth is not the only planet in the universe, Jacob. I guess you'll just have to open a door to a world where we'll come out above ground."

A renewed hope surged through me. "Tell me how."

The thirty seconds Bringelkoopf spent collecting his thoughts and slithering up my arm to perch on my shoulder were among the most agonizing of my life. I barely noticed that he clicked his claws in unison with my flicking fingers. Or that when he spoke, we both stopped simultaneously.

"Ok, here goes..." He took a deep breath and spoke with a soft reverence. "There is an almost spiritual connection between universes, which many species call—"

"Music," I whispered with a sudden burst of insight. Michael had said that music was Portalia's strength. I just hadn't realized the significance at the time.

"Yes, my friend. Music. It is the language of the soul. It is also how universes communicate and connect with each other. When the right music is played, its vibrations interact with the fabric of universes, allowing them to communicate with each other. And a powerful enough music can manipulate that fabric to forge a connection, or doorway, between them."

I thought about Grolfshin's quest to find kids with musical talent. Suddenly I had no doubt that my father had been right and that Harold the Duke of Vorkalis was not from Portalia. He was using Grolfshin to find a port and I was pretty certain it would not be good for Earth, or Portalia, if he succeeded.

There was a lot more at stake than me, Sammy, and Milokah, and his sister. A lot more."Okay, but what am I supposed to do? I don't have an instrument to play."

"And aren't we all grateful for that."

"What's that supposed to mean?"

"Do you really want me to tell you?"

"Well, how am I supposed to open a port without an instrument?"

"Why must you humans make it so complicated? It isn't the music you hear that opens the port, Jacob, it is the music from your soul that does. It is not created by instruments or voices. Those are simply the tools that humans use to play it.

"When your soul plays music, you hear the music in your head and your mind puts out brain waves that can interact with the universe much the same way sound waves interact with your eardrums."

Bringelkoopf's tone became somber. "What you need to understand, Jacob, is that the port you opened in your clubhouse was an existing port. It is one thing to open an existing port, and quite another to build a new one. That kind of talent," he added, with a vague wave of his tail, "is not so common."

Talent. My heart plummeted. Talent was one thing I did not have. But we didn't have the luxury of waiting until I grew into my ears. I was all we had. And I had to try.

"So, what do I do?"

"To sing the song of souls, you must be in harmony with yourself, one player, one voice, singing one song."

That made absolutely no sense to me. I waited for Bringelkoopf to explain. But he didn't. In fact, he became eerily quiet. My mouth went suddenly very dry.

"You don't know, do you?"

Bringelkoopf shook his head. "Your father was evasive about it. He told me that in order for his heart to resonate with his soul, he first had to tune it with the right key."

"What does that mean?"

"I don't know. I think it was something Piltan taught him."

"Who's Piltan?"

Bringelkoopf responded with a dismissive wave of his tail. "The thing is, Jacob, you already figured out how to do it, you just don't realize it."

"But I haven't figured anything out."

"Yes, you have. You had to have. Or else you wouldn't be here. Last night when you were telling us about how you got here, you remembered something. I could see it on your face, you smiled, and for a second..." Bringelkoopf choked on a sob. "You looked so like your father. But you didn't tell us what it was. You were hiding it from us. But whatever it was, that was it."

Then he did the strangest thing. He rested his forehead against mine and tweaked my hair with a gentleness that proved he was capable of using his claws without causing pain.

"You are a small boy, Jacob, with the biggest ears I've ever seen, and the biggest soul I've ever felt. You are your father's son, my young friend, and I have faith in you."

It might have been a moment. A moment to treasure forever.

But just then, I heard muffled voices from above the dungeon stairs. One sounded very much like the gravelly voice of a man with a red beard and yellow eyes.

Bringelkoopf tensed. "Jacob, you need to do this, and you need to do this *now*. Just remember, try to find a planet above ground, not below. Think air, not dirt."

An icy hand gripped my heart. Ready or not, Bringelkoopf's lesson on porting was over.

BREAKING FREE

IT WAS THE SMILE. The thing I'd hidden from Michael and the others. The smile, and the moment of love, beauty, and hope that I'd captured to keep safely in my soul forever.

I tried to think of the smile again.

But no matter how hard I tried, I could no longer see the smile from my dreams.

All I could see was Milokah's smile, as it was in the meadow when we danced.

My soul quivered. And an eerie tingle ran down my spine.

Not for the first time, I realized that Milokah's smile had looked exactly like the smile in my dreams. Only better.

And suddenly I knew. Milokah was my key. The one to tune my heart.

I forced aside the agonizing memory of the way I'd hurt him, and thought only of his eyes, and his smile, and how very much I loved him. Milokah struck a chord inside me. He resonated with my soul so intensely that its vibrations coursed throughout my entire body.

Reminding myself to think air, not dirt, I sang with my soul from the highest mountain peaks within me. My soul responded with music so loud that everyone in the castle should have been able to hear it.

The wall of my cell began to shimmer. I leapt into it and immediately found myself blanketed in sunlight.

Hope washed over me and I started to think that I might actually be able to rescue us after all. I hopped to the left, eager to open a port to Sammy's cell, for his was the closest to the approaching voices.

Bringelkoopf stopped me. "Don't forget to close the port behind you. And before you ask, no, I don't know how."

Without even thinking, I lifted my hand and flicked my wrist. Just like that, the shimmer disappeared. I didn't have time to congratulate myself. Instead, my thoughts turned to my best friend, stranded in the darkness of his cell. My soul responded with music as obnoxious and vile as the dungeon.

As soon as I sensed the air shimmering, I dashed through and was assaulted by a wave of the all-too-familiar putrid dungeon smell.

My toe stubbed against something soft and I heard a yelp of surprise from Sammy.

The footsteps and voices were getting closer.

Grabbing Sammy's arm I flung us both back through the shimmer. The moment my foot hit the grassy hilltop, I spun and slammed the port shut.

"I'll be right back," I told Sammy.

I darted to my left and thought of Milokah. Opening ports was getting easier and easier.

"Jacob, wait," Bringelkoopf said.

"Not now, there's no time."

Bringelkoopf dug his claws into my shoulder to get my attention. But the shimmer appeared and I jumped without waiting to hear what he had to say. A mistake I quickly regretted.

I'd ported to an empty cell.

I gulped. Where was I? More important, where was Milokah? I couldn't call out to him, Harold and Grolfshin were getting closer, so I tapped Bringelkoopf's tail and he coasted down quietly and snuck away.

"I will have that port tonight, Prios," Harold growled. "I'll give you five minutes. After that I'm more than happy to get it myself."

Grolfshin rushed to reassure him. "No, no, that won't be necessary. He will tell me. I'm sure of it."

By the time Bringelkoopf clawed his way back up my shoulder, Grolfshin and Harold were so close that I could hear the soft rustling of Grolfshin's cloak, and smell the horse sweat still clinging to it.

I froze, certain that Grolfshin and Harold would hear any motion on my part.

"One cell to the right," Bringelkoopf whispered. "Quick. You must do it now."

Yes, I thought, now would be good. But my brain was enclosed in a dense fog. I'd become arrogant and ended up in the wrong cell. Now I was unable to move, unable to think, and certainly unable to sing a song with my soul.

Just then, the footsteps skidded to a halt.

"Jacob—guards!" Grolfshin had found my empty cell.

Just then, a loud, heart-wrenching groan came from the next cell over.

I wondered how many children my uncle had ripped from their mothers' arms and a fierce determination exploded in me. My body unfroze, and my brain fog shattered like shards of glass. I sang a desperate song with my soul, a plea for an unborn child's freedom.

The wall shimmered and I hurtled through. My feet were still in midair as I slammed the port shut with a mental flick of my wrist. I didn't even glance at Sammy. I vaulted to the side and my soul again called out to Portalia. I waited, tense with the fear that I would be too late.

When I saw a brief flicker, I dove through before the shimmer had fully expanded. It was like squeezing through a too-small tunnel. The intense pressure constricted my chest and forced the air painfully from my lungs. But I didn't care.

The ear-splitting wail of Grolfshin's angry outburst assailed me. "Where is that little scoundrel? How did he get out? The boy, the girl, check them."

Grabbing blindly for the nearest arm, I tossed the person on the end of it towards the portal. Her yelp of surprise was cut off as she disappeared safely through to the other side.

As I was reaching for another arm, Grolfshin slid into view, illuminated by the light of his lantern. He gaped in disbelief and momentarily forgot the keychain he gripped in his other hand.

Milokah caught my eyes, and for a split second I knew we shared the same thought. His sister and her baby were safe. I could close the port now and they would remain safe. It was a comforting thought, but we both knew it wasn't the right answer.

Seconds later, Harold oozed into view, a coiled rope dangling from his fist. The bizarre rope was entwined with chunks of ivory and tufts of hair. I didn't give it a second thought.

All I could think about were Harold's eyes. They were not filled with disbelief. They were filled with pure, undiluted anger. And they were calling out to me.

I swayed and took a step toward him.

Harold curled his lips into an all-knowing, smug, triumphant grin.

In the back of my mind, I knew we should be escaping through the port. Except that would upset Harold, and suddenly, I did not want to upset Harold.

Something tugged at me. Milokah was saying something, my name I think. But his voice was hollow and sounded miles away and it didn't have the pull that Harold's eyes did.

Those yellow, haunting eyes. They captivated me. I stepped once again toward them.

At the edge of my vision, I saw Grolfshin fumbling with the keychain. When he found the key, he would unlock the cell. And if we were still standing here, Harold would have us.

And we would still be standing here. Because although my soul yearned to take Milokah to safety, my eyes could not break from Harold's, and my feet refused to move away

"Jacob!" Bringelkoopf yelled in my ear. "We need to go, now!"

Two things happened then to spur me on.

First, Bringelkoopf bit a large chunk of my ear. The pain was excruciating. One could even say it was distracting.

I screeched in agony. As I did, my eyes were torn away from Harold's hypnotic hold. They moved all the way over to Grolfshin and watched him lifting a key.

That's when the second thing happened.

As Grolfshin looked down to insert the key into the lock, a tear rolled down his cheek. I didn't know what had caused my uncle to shed a tear at that moment. But something about it moved me, and gave me the strength to resist Harold. And just in time.

"Jacob," Harold called to me, cajoling me with his soft, lulling, oh-so-wonderful voice.

"Don't look," warned Bringelkoopf. His teeth grazed my ear, ready to strike again if needed.

But I needed no warning. With a speed that amazed me, I grabbed Milokah's arm.

Grolfshin drove the key into the lock while Harold uncoiled the bizarre rope and positioned himself, ready to throw the grate open.

Sometimes, ignorance is bliss. And sometimes, ignorance—like not knowing that the rope in Harold's hand had the power to bring destruction to all of humanity—is the only thing that allows a scared kid to be brave.

I plucked Milokah up as though he were merely one of his delightful strands of wavy jet-black hair and casually flung him through the shimmer.

Grolfshin turned the key.

I observed as if watching from a distant place.

The lock slid open with a heavy, dull clank.

A tear fell from Grolfshin's chin and splashed onto his hand.

Harold heaved against the grate and the ground trembled beneath his massive weight.

The smirk on my face appeared of its own. I barely knew it was there. I looked up in defiance and locked eyes with my enemy.

My eyes dared him to try once more to hypnotize me. My chest swelled with the desire of my soul to speak, to tell Harold that I would make him pay for the pain he had caused my family and my people. There was no need for words. He got my message.

"Prios!" His voice was shrill above the grate's creaking hinges. He barged in and threw a loop of his bizarre rope at me like a lasso.

I flung myself backwards, but his rope ensnared my foot. He yanked viciously, and I stared in horrified panic as the rope tightened around my ankle.

I scrambled and clawed at the moldy ground, desperately seeking a grip for my fingers so they could haul me towards the shimmer, which was just beyond my reach.

Harold jerked me towards him and laughed. He laughed because he could. He'd caught me. And he knew it. In fact, he knew it so well that he got careless. He was less than ten feet from me. Two of his long strides and he could have had me. Two strides and he would have won.

Instead, he played with me, like a cat plays with a ball of yarn. His yellow eyes danced as he watched me fight a futile game of tug-of-war with a man three times my size.

The problem for the cat is that the cat thinks it knows exactly what the ball of yarn is going to do, which is nothing. Can you imagine the look on the cat's face if the ball of yarn were to spring to life and start moving on its own? I didn't have to imagine. I was about to find out.

I swiveled my gaze to Grolfshin. Keeping my eyes locked with his, I stopped fighting against the rope and waited for the right moment. I did not have to wait long.

With the cat's smug certainty that the ball of yarn has been well and truly conquered, Harold relaxed his grip. Only for a fraction of a second. But that was all I needed.

Mustering strength from every fiber in my body, I propelled myself towards the shimmer.

I did not take the time to savor the startled cry from Harold as the rope slipped through his hands. Nor did I relish his look of shock that must resemble the poor cat's when the ball of yarn moves without permission.

Instead, I kept my eyes riveted to my uncle's and scampered through the portal.

One minute, I was staring at Grolfshin. The next I was blinded by searing light. The warmth of the blazing sun washed over me. First my face. Then my chest. Then my legs.

But before it reached my feet, it stopped. The rope around my ankle tightened and began dragging my body back through the port. To Harold.

"Quick, help me," I called out, grasping frantically at the grass.

Sammy and Milokah pounced on my wrists and hauled with all their might.

"Close the port!" shrieked Bringelkoopf. "Close it now!"

A searing pain radiated up my leg. My body was stretched so taut that I wondered if it were possible to be pulled in half. "Pull harder!"

"We're trying!" Sammy said.

"Close the port! Close it now!" Bringelkoopf roared. "Close the port, Jacob!"

I wanted desperately to do exactly that. But I also wanted desperately to keep my foot. And my foot was still on the other side. Then a black-gloved hand reached through and grabbed my ankle and I realized I had no choice. Clenching my teeth, I willed the port to shut.

The shimmer collapsed all the way down to my foot, then snapped back open with a vengeance. I stared in horror. I'd willed it to shut but it had not.

Distraught, I willed it even harder. I no longer cared about my foot. I wanted only to close the port and keep evil away. The shimmer collapsed to my ankle with a snap. Again it stopped. It smoked, it sizzled, and it crackled. But it would not close.

The gloved hand retracted, leaving behind smoking fragments of black leather.

The shimmer hovered around the rope. The rope which was still attached to my ankle and still trying to pull me back.

To fight my rising panic I took myself back to that moment in the meadow. With Milokah. Only then did it occur to me that Milokah was right in front of me, gripping my arm. Pulling with Sammy. Trying to save me.

I slid my eyes up my right arm until they reached my wrist, and a hand a shade darker than mine. Then I lifted them another fraction, and locked eyes with Milokah. There were a thousand things I wanted to say to him, but I forced myself to shove them aside.

Instead, I looked into his eyes, and into him. From deep within me, something powerful surged. And though I knew not what it was, my soul sang that something powerful. And that something powerful burst through me and did what I had failed to do before.

The ground rattled violently and the portal collapsed with a loud, deafening crack.

A miniature smoke-filled tornado blasted forth, catapulting me into the air and spitting out singed fragments of the bizarre rope.

I landed several yards away. A chunk of ivory thudded into the ground beside me.

"You all right?" Sammy and Milokah stood over me, their faces etched with concern.

My head was spinning, my ears were ringing, and I couldn't remember how to speak.

But when I wiggled my toes, they were still there, along with the feet to which they were still attached. That seemed like a good thing, so I nodded.

The nod was a mistake. The small movement made the ache behind my eyeballs worse.

Unfortunately, I quickly discovered it wasn't safe to close my eyes, just yet. Instead, I picked up the discarded remnant of ivory and rolled it in my fingers. The texture was soothing and calming, and distracted me from my pain.

"Dude, I can't believe you did that," Sammy said.

"Me neither," Bringelkoopf said.

Milokah said nothing.

Eventually, my world stopped spinning enough that I closed my eyes to rest.

Everywhere I turned, people seemed to be placing their hopes in me. Sammy, Milokah, Bringelkoopf, they'd all placed their hopes in me.

But in the last two days, never had I expected to see hope where I'd just seen it—in the eyes of my father's only brother. The uncle I'd never known I had. The man who had tossed me in a dungeon.

I'd closed my eyes to rest. But rest was not what I got. What I got was a memory of the look on Grolfshin's tear-stained face just before I went through the port.

The last thing I'd seen as I escaped from the dungeon was my uncle, looking at his scrawny nephew, with pride. And hope.

And that gave me hope.

FREEDOM'S GIFT

AFTER A FEW minutes, I managed to stand up, blink, and even speak without too much pain.

Milokah introduced me to his sister, Teleana, who thanked me profusely for rescuing them.

I didn't know what to say, especially since I was the reason they'd been in danger in the first place. Despite the horrible way I'd treated him, Milokah had still brought his sister to me to put her salve on the scrapes on my side. They'd walked right into Grolfshin's hands.

Fortunately, nobody seemed to mind that I wasn't talkative. Or that I wandered off to be alone for a few minutes and revel in the safety and beauty of this warm and sunny world.

We had stepped into a painting. The kind you expect to see in a museum.

On every side were rolling hills dotted with yellow trees and carpeted with fluorescent green grass that glittered beneath the orange glow of the setting sun.

The star-shaped trees had orange tendrils that jutted upwards, dangling juicy, basketball-sized red globes from their tips.

A gentle breeze scooped tiny granules from the surface of the globes and floated them across to us. They had a faint lemony scent that created a strange yearning within me.

But I didn't have time to wonder at the scent because my eyes and thoughts were drawn upwards to a huge bird flying straight toward us. He was as big as a horse and looked exactly like an American bald eagle.

When he was almost upon me, he veered sharply and perched on a tree not ten feet away.

I gulped, or rather, I tried to. He was not only very, very big, but he also had very, very big talons. Naturally, I mean, who expects a huge eagle to have small talons? Probably only me.

He plucked a globe from its tendril and swallowed it almost whole. I say almost, because a small fragment sheared off, leaving behind a red ooze. I couldn't help but notice that the ooze was the color of blood, and that the globe had been bigger than my head.

When he finished the remnants, the eagle swiveled his eyes toward me.

Bringelkoopf promptly scooted down the back of my shirt. I glanced over my shoulder and saw that all my friends were stashed just as safely behind me as my not-a-ferret friend. I wished I had someone to hide behind. After all, hiding was my super talent.

But it was clear that my new role as savior, people's hope, and brave warrior had been universally accepted by everyone. Including Sammy.

After a few heart-thumping moments, the eagle hopped down and took a few steps toward me. I did the same and we approached each other warily. Although I could not quite figure out why *he* would be wary.

Even so, I stretched out my hand and said, "It's okay." Because that's what you say to frightened wild animals, right? And surely it worked just as well when you were the frightened animal in question?

It was another of those moments I would look back upon as a sign that things had already changed between Sammy and me. Two days earlier, Sammy would never have watched while his snack-sized best friend walked up to an enormous bird of prey with an outstretched hand.

When I reached the eagle, he craned his head until his beak touched his chest so that he could look at me.

As I gazed up into his eyes, a peaceful calm washed over me and I remembered something Rick had said just before the twins were born when he took me and Sammy on a picnic. We saw an eagle soaring overhead and Rick told us that the eagle was the symbol of freedom. Tears had streamed down his face as he watched the majestic bird and Sammy and I had been confused about why he was crying. We were eight.

But as I stared up into the penetrating eyes of that magnificent ambassador of freedom, I was no longer confused.

My chest brushed against his and his warm, moist breath blew the hair off my face like a bellows. His feathers had a musky, lemony scent, like the fruit from the trees, and I vaguely wondered what I smelled like to him.

Stretching up onto the very tips of my toes and rested my fingers on his beak. It was as smooth as glass. A tingle radiated from his beak, through my hand, and into my entire being. He had sensed my need, and willingly poured a share of his strength into me. I accepted it eagerly.

Once he'd refueled me, my hand slipped away.

As soon as I broke our connection, he took two strides, unfolded his vast wings and set himself aloft with seamless, majestic strokes. My eyes followed him into the distance. Just before he disappeared, I whispered, "Freedom. Your name is Freedom."

I wanted nothing more than to remain frozen in that moment forever, but my thoughts were interrupted by a cry of agony from Teleana. She was going to have her baby soon. I had to find a way back to Portalia, and preferably one that did not lead us right into Harold's eagerly outstretched hands.

Bringelkoopf popped up from his hiding place and nudged my ear. I'm not convinced it was an accident that he nudged the same ear he'd taken a bite out of earlier.

"So, what now?" he asked.

"We need to get to Michael's."

"I agree! I don't know about you, but I could use a nice bowl of stew."

At the mention of stew, my stomach growled. And as I gazed in the direction Freedom had flown, I thought I caught a whiff of cinnamon, apples, and something else on the breeze. As if Freedom was wafting the aroma to me with his mighty wings.

I glanced over at Sammy, Milokah, and Teleana.

They were all looking at me expectantly.

So, pretending a confidence I didn't feel I said, "This way," and strode boldly forward.

They followed me without question.

I took us over several rolling hills, drawn inexplicably towards a small cluster of globe-less trees. When we got there, I felt it. A feeling of warmth and safety. I thought of Milokah's smile, and the tree beside us shimmered.

I went first to make sure it was safe.

Strangely, I was the only one surprised to discover that I'd managed to bring us all back to a safe spot on Portalia, not too far from Michael's.

As we walked towards the comfort and safety of Michael's, I thought back to that final moment in the dungeon, and the look on my uncle's face. I did not know what my uncle hoped for. But I knew what I hoped for.

I hoped against all hope that my uncle had seen the tears running down my own face. And maybe, just maybe, he would know that I loved him.

More to comfort myself than anyone else, I socked Sammy on the shoulder. He smiled, and thumped me back. Not as hard as I would have liked. Not as hard as he used to.

I knew then that Sammy and I would never be the same again.

A huge weight settled on my shoulders, so heavy I expected my legs to buckle beneath me at any moment. But they didn't.

Instead, I strode onwards toward Michael's, not realizing that with every step I took, I was growing little by little into my father's ears. Filled with a strength gifted to me by Freedom himself, step by step, I walked towards my destiny, and the destiny of all my people.

HONOR THE MEMORY

WITH THE PROMISE of safety, security, and food in his future, Sammy's good spirits and inquisitive nature returned. "Bringelkoopf?" he asked. "What happens if a port closes when somebody's halfway through?"

Bringelkoopf snickered. "What do you think, Buttercup? Do you think you can live with only half your body?"

"No."

"Well then, you don't need to be a brain surgeon to figure that one out, do you?"

I thought about the black gloved hand that had been around my ankle and shuddered. Then I remembered something. "Hey, Bringelkoopf?"

"Hey, Jacob?"

"When Sammy said he couldn't believe I'd done it, you said you couldn't either. But you were the one who'd told me I could do it in the first place. What did you mean?"

Bringelkoopf fidgeted and squirmed and rearranged himself. But he said nothing until I tugged at his tail.

He spoke reluctantly. "I didn't *think* you could, Jacob, but I *hoped* you could."

"You *hoped* I could?" I shrieked. "*That* was your brilliant escape plan?"

"Well, it worked, didn't it?" He tweaked my hair. "And I was right, wasn't I? Now, if you don't mind, I need a nap."

With that, he settled down and promptly fell asleep.

As the five of us walked toward Michael's—or rather, four of us walked while the fifth slept, curled up on my shoulders—I felt strangely alone. I wanted to turn to Sammy, as I'd always done. Except that I couldn't, because I knew that if I did, I'd start to cry.

I'd met Sammy at my father's memorial service. He'd thrown a protective arm around me and said, "Come on, Jakey, let's go outside. Too many big people in here."

We'd been inseparable ever since.

Once he took a dog bite for me. It was after Rocco died. I'd seen Sparky over in Mr. Mortenson's yard with a ball in his mouth. I had thought that all dogs loved to have you take the ball out of their mouth to play toss and fetch, like Rocco had.

I had thought wrong. Seventeen stitches to Sammy's right shin wrong.

Then there was the time at the lake when I took my lifejacket off because it was too scratchy. Not two seconds later, I fell into the water and couldn't keep my head above the surface. Sammy jumped in and pulled me out.

Unfortunately, that was only two days after the ball misunderstanding with Sparky, and Sammy's seventeen stitches got infected from the nasty lake water.

I had hundreds of stories like that. But those days were over now.

We stopped for Teleana and I glanced over at Sammy. He and Milokah were doing their best to help Teleana. Her contractions were getting stronger and we were stopping more frequently.

Milokah looked up and smiled at me. His smile was sad and tentative and I couldn't bear it, that I'd caused him such pain. He was so close, yet so far away. But he was only far away because I'd put him there.

Milokah had done more than simply make my heart flutter and my skin tingle. He'd connected with the deepest depths of my soul.

I replayed every second of our final moments in the meadow. The way I'd leapt up at the sight of Sammy. The way I'd bolted away from him when he'd moved towards me. The way I'd told Sammy that Milokah was nobody, just some kid.

Milokah hadn't had to hear me say those things to know I'd said them. The pain on his face told me that.

I'd been hiding all my life. But until now I'd never hurt anybody else by doing it.

I didn't know when, or if, I'd get a chance to talk to Milokah alone, without Sammy. All I knew was that I had to make things right, no matter what. I had to be true to him. And I had to be true to myself. Even if I was still figuring out what that meant.

Then I thought of Freedom, and the strength he'd gifted me. I took a deep breath, and spoke the words before I could coward my way out of them. "Hey, Milokah, can I talk to you for a minute?"

"Yeah, sure."

I watched to see how Sammy would react. But Sammy didn't hear me, he was too busy plying Teleana with his charming antics to distract her from her pain. He didn't seem to notice that Milokah had left him alone to tend to his sister while he came to talk to me.

"Hey." Milokah's voice, like his smile, was hesitant.

"I'm sorry," I blurted. "He doesn't know yet, and I... I'm really, really sorry."

Milokah glanced over his shoulder at Sammy.

"I'm really sorry," I said again. "I never meant to hurt you."

"It's okay," he said. "I get it, sort of, I think." He spoke the words as if he was trying to make his heart believe them.

"Yeah?" I asked, daring to hope.

In answer, Milokah shuffled closer and reached for my hand.

It took every shred of willpower I'd never known I had to keep from pulling back. Sammy was only ten feet away. But I knew that if I pulled away now, I'd lose Milokah. Nothing in the universe was worth that.

Instead, I turned my hand palm up so that he could place his in it.

As soon as I did, he burst into a happy smile that made my heart leap. "I forgive you, but only because you apologized twice." And because you didn't pull away, his eyes added.

"Thanks."

"I still brought my sister to put her salve on your side, didn't I?"

And if he hadn't, if he'd turned his back on me like I had him, he and Teleana wouldn't be here now. They'd be somewhere safe.

"I'm so sorry." The words seemed more inadequate each time I uttered them.

"Don't be. That part, at least, wasn't your fault."

He squeezed my hand when I started to protest. "It's okay, really. I mean it."

Then he let go and went back to Teleana and Sammy.

Just before we started walking again, he let me look into his eyes once more. It felt just like it had when I'd looked into Freedom's eyes and refueled. Only better.

I realized then that I had to tell Sammy. Until I stopped hiding, I'd never be free. Before that moment, it had never occurred to me that I couldn't both hide, and be free, at the same time.

But I would have to wait to talk to Sammy. He and Milokah were both busy with Teleana.

So I decided to try to remember what else had happened that day my father and Grolfshin had fought.

* * *

As soon as they pulled into the driveway Rocco leapt from the car and ran around the front yard doing his happy dance. Little Me didn't notice. All he knew was that he found himself suddenly squashed between Mommie and Daddie.

"You're back early," Mommie said. "Did everything go okay?"

Daddie set Little Me down. "Go play with Rocco, Jakey."

Little Me knew right away that something was wrong. He wanted to stay and listen but he couldn't ignore his friend's slurping tongue. But as he tossed the ball for his eager buddy, Little Me kept his eyes and ears focused on Mommie and Daddie.

"I am not going back there," Mommie said, "and neither is Jacob. He's only four."

"But my brother needs me."

"Your son needs you. Your wife needs you," Mommie said. Then she folded her arms. That was a very bad sign.

"I have a duty to my people," Daddie said. "Can't you see that? I never meant to be away for so long. It's my home. You knew that when you married me."

"That was before Jacob was born. It's your world, Prantos, not his."

"No, Laney, you're wrong. It is his world. And his destiny. You cannot change who he is just by hiding him here on Earth. He is going to be their King someday."

"Not if your brother has any say in it. If you need to go, then go, but Jacob stays here."

"Okay." Daddie nodded sadly. "I'll go without him. I'll finish the clubhouse with him today."

Mommie and Daddie hugged then and Little Me ran to them and wrapped his arms around their legs. They each took half of the tangled black mop on his head and competed to see who could get their side straightened out first. Little Me loved that game. It was why he hated having his hair cut. Because when it was short, there was nothing for Mommie and Daddie to untangle on his head.

Later that day, after Little Me and his dad finished the clubhouse they sat on top and enjoyed their end-of-the-working-day rituals.

Daddie ran a handkerchief across his forehead to wipe off the sweat and Little Me copied him with his very own handkerchief.

It was a hot day, but the sweat on Daddie's forehead was not from the heat. It was from a day spent pounding nails, hauling wood planks, and climbing up and down a ladder.

Little Me, on the other hand, had spent his day carefully handing nails to his father. A task which did not cause his forehead to sprout beads of sweat. He wiped his forehead anyway.

After the brow-wiping ritual, the rest-and-recovery ritual started.

Little Me snuggled up against his dad and closed his eyes and listened.

First Daddie rifled through ice cubes, hunting for the perfect can.

Next Daddie flicked the can and popped the tab open.

Then Daddie guzzled the fuzzy goodness with a very precise tempo of glug, glug, aaaaah.

When there were only two or three sips of soda left, Daddie handed the can to his son.

Little Me clutched the can between his tiny hands and took tiny sips and Daddie said the same thing he always said. "Don't tell Mom about the soda, okay?"

Little Me giggled. They both knew that Mom already knew.

Then his father told him a story.

It was Little Me's favorite story, because as his Dad spoke, his voice always rose and fell, like waves on the ocean, sweeping Little Me away to a cozy, happy place.

Except this time, the waves of his dad's voice were choppy and they did not sweep him away to a cozy place. And Daddie's body shook as he choked out the final words. "Upon his arrival, Portalia will rejoice and sing, for he is her guardian, the portal master, and most of all, her people's King."

Then Daddie did something that was definitely not part of their ritual. He buried his face in Little Me's hair and cried.

Suddenly the screen door slammed and Mommie came outside with a strange man.

The strange man had a beard like Santa Claus, except that otherwise he was nothing like Santa Claus. His beard was red. And even from a distance Little Me could tell that the strange man was not a nice man.

But what Little Me really couldn't understand was why his mom had not gotten mad at the man for slamming the door. Mommie very, very did not like slamming doors.

Daddie spun Little Me around and held him close. "Jacob, never forget that Daddie loves you. Never forget that you are a Prios and that you have a destiny."

With that, his father left him and went down to Mommie and the strange man.

"What are you doing here, Felix?" Daddie asked.

The strange man was twirling a hairy rope with white chunks woven in it. He had scary, yellow eyes and his laugh made Little Me's skin crawl.

"I should have done it when I came through," the man said. "That was my mistake. No matter. You will take me."

Little Me very, very did not like that man. Rocco didn't either. But Rocco was trapped inside the house. He pawed and scratched madly at the screen door, but the door did not budge. Because just last week, Daddie had finally put a sturdy latch on it like Mommie had asked him to. Daddie had promised Mommie that Rocco could no longer open it. He'd been right.

Rocco was livid. His lips were pulled back, his fangs were bared and he snarled viciously. He looked nothing like Little Me's most favorite naptime pillow.

The man glanced meaningfully up at Little Me. "Show me the port, Prantos. Show it to me *now*."

"Okay, Felix, okay. I'll show you, but they stay here."

"I don't think so, Prantos."

"Then you can find it yourself."

The strange man shrugged. "Okay. It doesn't matter anyway."

Daddie ushered the man to his car. He paused before getting in, and gazed up at his son. Little Me couldn't understand the strange look on Daddie's face as he mouthed, "Goodbye, I love you."

Then Daddie drove away.

Little Me stretched out his tiny hand. "No, Daddie, don't go with that man. Jakey very, very doesn't like him, and Rocco doesn't either."

But it was too late. The car turned the corner. And his father was gone. Forever.

The next day Little Me was in the kitchen, toying with a sandwich that he and Rocco didn't feel like eating when there was a heavy rap at the front door.

Mommie opened the door and a policeman stepped inside. He said something that Little Me couldn't hear and Mommie began howling.

When the howling stopped, the policeman spoke, this time a little louder. "Mrs. Prios, I'm sorry for your loss. But the man with your husband had no ID. Do you know who he is?"

"Is he dead too?" Mommie asked.

"Yes. Do you know his name? So we can notify his family?"

"No, I don't, and I don't care. Goodbye."

In the blink of an eye, Mommie pulled herself together. She pushed the bewildered policeman out and slammed the door. Then she came to Rocco and Little Me and gathered them into a hug. She did not cry. She did not say a word.

And she hadn't spoken of Daddie since.

* * *

A tree branch thwacked against my forehead and brought me back to the present. My heart ached as if it was just yesterday that I'd watched my father drive away.

A twitchy whisker tickled my ear. I reached up to scratch Bringelkoopf's furry chin, earning myself a very cat-like purr from the not-a-ferret who insisted he was not a pet.

"How much longer?" I asked when we stopped yet again for Teleana.

"We still have a way to go, but we should be there in half an hour." Bringelkoopf glanced skeptically at Teleana. "Or maybe a bit longer."

"Do you think that will be soon enough?"

"Don't worry Jacob, she's a strong woman, and...."

"And?"

"Let's just say she's had a hard life and leave it at that for now, okay?"

"Okay."

I thought it fitting that the sun was just beginning to set as we continued on to Michael's. Because for me, the sun was setting on everything I'd thought I'd known to be true about my father.

When I'd watched my father drive away, I could not have known that it would not be until I was walking on a strange planet in a parallel universe eight years later that I would finally understand the strange look on his face as he mouthed goodbye to me.

It was the look of a man who knew he would not be coming back.

My father's death was no accident. My father had never abandoned his people. My father had sacrificed himself to protect his family and his people from evil.

For the accident that took my father's life also took the life of the man called Felix, a man with a red beard and haunting yellow eyes. A man just like Harold.

I wanted to scream at the injustice. I could not bring myself to believe that the simple act of changing the latch on a screen door may have been the thing that doomed my father.

But the very last thing my father had said to me was that I had a destiny. Whatever that destiny was, I knew one thing. If I accomplished nothing else in life, I would make sure my father did not die in vain.

COMFORT OF MICHAEL'S

MICHAEL RUMMAGED FRANTICALLY through his cupboards.
The tension in the cabin was on the verge of exploding when he finally leapt up clutching a green bottle. "Ah, here it is."
In one fluid motion, he popped it open, sending its cork flying, and filled a mug with its sludgy green liquid.
Even from across the room, the vapors caused my eyes to water. It smelled like something you have to pin someone down, pinch their nose tight, and lie through your teeth about how nasty it really isn't, to get them to swallow.
Michael set the foul concoction in front of Teleana. "This will help," he told her, foregoing the whole inconvenient lying-through-his-teeth part in favor of not saying anything at all about the taste.
Not that it mattered. Teleana took one whiff, gagged, and shoved it aside.
Whether it was because I had spent so much time in protection mode, or because I was simply just that clueless, I don't know. But without thinking I blurted, "What is that? Are you sure it's safe? She's having a baby. It won't hurt the baby, will it?"
"Really?" Bringelkoopf said. "A baby? You don't say!"
Teleana glared at me. Sammy buried his face in his hands. And Milokah looked like he might burst with laughter.
Yep, definitely clueless, I decided.
Michael chuckled. "Yes, Jacob, I know she's having a baby. It is safe. It did not harm your mother, or you, for that matter."
"Me?" It had never occurred to me that I was born on Portalia.
Michael winked at me and put a hand on Teleana's back.

"Go on, dear, it's not that bad." He was clearly better at lying than I would have liked.

Teleana tossed Michael a dubious look before quickly and bravely gulping it down. By the look on her face, it tasted even worse than it smelled.

"There. You should start to feel better soon," Michael said. He turned to Milokah. "Milo, dear, take Telly to the bedroom. I'll send for Ma Korsen."

Just before the door closed behind him and Teleana, Milokah turned and gave me a smile that melted my heart. Then he was gone.

As soon as the door swung shut, Michael collected me into a bear hug.

He whispered into my hair, as if savoring the memory. "Yes, Jacob, you were born right here, eleven years, three hundred sixty-four days and twenty hours ago."

My scalp tingled from his breath, and the rumble of his chest against mine reminded me of Freedom. I melted into his arms, and for a few blissful moments, he was the grandfather I'd never had. I wanted to cement my arms around him forever. Like Freedom and Milokah, he refueled me with something I so desperately needed. Comfort.

"I delivered you myself. You were so eager to be born that you refused to wait for Ma. She was most displeased with you."

With a sigh, he pulled away from me and trotted towards the entry steps.

"Speaking of which," he called over his shoulder, "I'd best send for Breskin and Ma. Ma will have my head on a platter if she misses Telly's delivery."

He didn't sound exactly scared of Ma, but he seemed especially eager not to upset her.

My fingers twitched as he disappeared.

"Don't worry yourself into a tizzy. He'll be right back," Bringelkoopf said. He stretched and yawned, then slipped down from my shoulders to curl up in a contented ball near the fire.

He was right. The next thing I knew, Michael was back. He flew to the hearth, slowing in mid-stride only long enough to give Sammy an affectionate pat on the back before captivating us with a flawless performance of his stew-serving ritual.

Sammy was in heaven. A bowl of stew and all his fear and anxiety vanished.

Michael set a small bowl in front of Bringelkoopf and scratched him behind the ears. "It was very peaceful and quiet last night."

"Hmph, I missed you too, you old goat." Bringelkoopf gave Michael a playful nip before he began a very Sammy-like process of food inhalation.

Michael left Bringelkoopf to his stew and joined me and Sammy at the table.

Sammy shuffled the food in his mouth around to make room for his tongue. "So, you got like homing pigeons or something?"

Michael's eyes crinkled with amusement. "Something like that, only a smidgeon bigger. And faster, with sharper claws. I'll show you one someday."

"Sweet." Sammy grinned.

Yes, food seemed to possess magical healing properties for Sammy and Bringelkoopf.

But although the orange mush and chewy bread soothed my aching stomach, they did nothing for my aching heart. Because somewhere deep inside, somehow I already knew that I was eating the last meal of my childhood.

When Michael had wiped his mug spotless and licked his fingers clean, Bringelkoopf dragged himself away from the crackling fire and perched at his elbow.

Together, they stared at me.

"Tell me what happened," Michael said.

His eyes were warm as I told him about how much I'd liked Grolfshin at first and how badly I'd wanted my uncle to love me back.

But as soon as I told him about our escape from the dungeon, everything changed. And I mean everything.

The pinpoints of light in his eyes exploded like supernovae, so vividly that I half-expected a shooting star to dart out and strike me. He and Bringelkoopf locked eyes with a skin-tingling intensity. Silently, they shared a very special secret. About me.

The secrecy was too much. "Tell me the truth," I said. "About my father, about Grolfshin, about Portalia. Please, just tell me."

"Okay, Jacob. Okay." Michael rose, grabbed the green bottle and headed toward the hall door. "But first, let me check on Telly. Then I'll tell you."

"Will you?"

Michael paused with his back to me. "Yes, Jacob, I will. I promise."

I was so caught up in my frustration that I didn't register the sadness in his voice. I was terrified that before he could come back some evil twist of fate, like an asteroid, would strike and he'd never answer all of my burning questions.

But there was no evil twist of fate, and Michael soon returned.

"How is she?" I asked. "And how's Milokah?"

"She's as well as she can be. She has a few more hours yet. And Milokah's fine."

"When's this Ma person going to get here?" Sammy asked.

"This Ma person should be here within the hour." Michael's shoulders shook with quiet laughter. "Though I suggest you not call her 'this Ma person.' She may not see the humor."

Michael topped up Sammy's bowl. Then he settled at the table with a large block of wood and a knife.

As soon as the knife appeared, Bringelkoopf bounded to Michael's feet and coiled up like a spring, bursting with eager anticipation. It didn't take me long to figure out why.

Michael glided his knife smoothly and easily, as though he were peeling a potato. He shaved a small layer here, a small layer there, sending slivers arcing gracefully outward with every stroke.

As he did, Bringelkoopf darted about the cabin in a blur, pouncing on the shavings the moment they touched the ground. He scooped them into a pile, then scattered them with a bizarre cackling purr of delight. It was a game, I suspected, that he and Michael had played a thousand times.

I'll never forget that warm and cozy night in Michael's cabin. The cadence of Michael's voice matched the rhythm of his hands and the sparkles in his eyes. The fire crackled in the background, filling the cabin with the pleasant scent of burning firewood while dancing flames cast shadows across Michael's face.

I perched on the edge of my seat, mesmerized, as Michael told me and Sammy a story.

At first I thought it was a story of Portalia. Then I realized it was a story about me. About my history. And my future.

It was a story about my destiny.

MY KINGDOM'S FOUNDATION

"**HUMANS ARE DREAMERS,** Jacob," Michael began. "They have a passion for life unlike any other species. For passion is the heart of humanity's soul, dreams are its voice, and the pursuit of those dreams is the breath of its very life.

"Exploration and discovery are essential for humans. And Portalia is meant to be the gateway through which they can spread their wings, pursue new dreams, connect with others, and infuse the breath of life into their very souls.

"But thousands of years ago, an act known as the Great Shutting separated Earth and Portalia, and forced humanity into seclusion. Humans have run out of opportunities for new exploration. Now they deny their passions. They ignore the voices of their souls, and they no longer pursue their dreams.

"Many believe the Great Shutting was an unforgivable act. Others felt the risk humanity posed warranted such interference. Either way, the consequences of the Great Shutting have been dire. The separation needs to end.

"Unless humans can relearn to hear the voices of their souls, their souls will wither and die like a plant that is not watered. And humanity with it. For the soul is the essence of life, and no species that has lost touch with its soul has ever survived.

"Before the Great Shutting, Portal Week was a joyous time when humans and other species traveled freely through permanent ports—portals that opened automatically at the beginning of the week and closed on their own at the end of the week. But the Great Shutters left no permanent ports open for humans and only four closed ports—portals that can be opened only with a very precise, and rare, talent.

"The primary port was in Egypt, at the Great Pyramid of Giza."

"I've always wanted to go to Egypt," Sammy said. His enthusiasm was short-lived.

Michael shook his head. "Three thousand years ago, a group of werewolf-like humans came through that port. They had an ability to control minds and used it to commit horrible acts. King Jacob the First was grieved. He could not allow them to remain, but he could not return them to Earth. So he banished them to another galaxy and asked to have the port at Giza shut."

"Guess Egypt's out," Sammy said.

"Who did he ask to shut the port?" I asked.

"The second port was at Stonehenge," Michael said, completely ignoring my question.

Sammy perked back up at the mention of Stonehenge. But Michael again shook his head.

"Five hundred years ago, the Helxin family went through that port and spent a year on Earth. When they returned, they'd gone mad. They killed hundreds of Portalians. King Prantos the Second banished them to another world. He worried that their madness was the result of a disease they'd picked up on Earth, so he asked to have that port shut as well."

"He asked who to shut the port?" I asked again.

"The third port," Michael said, again ignoring my question, "is the one your father used to use, Jacob."

"The one in Jacob's clubhouse?" Sammy asked.

"No," Michael said.

Sammy frowned, then tilted his head. "Do the closed ports only connect to one place?"

"Most are opened to only one destination, yes."

"Is that why the port from the dungeon went to that other place?" Sammy asked.

Michael winked and flipped a wood shaving into Sammy's lap.

Sammy smirked and swept the shaving into Bringelkoopf's pile. Nothing intrigued Sammy more than an adult's mysteriously unanswered question.

"So," Sammy continued, "what you're saying is, since the Great Shutting, hardly anybody can move between universes. And Portalians are the humans who were left behind on Portalia."

Michael nodded. "A handful of humans were selected to remain as Stewards of Portalia. From within them were selected the Guardians. And from within the Guardians, a family to form a royal lineage, from which all of Portalia's Kings would be descended."

"You said there were other species. What about them?" Sammy asked.

"Other than you and Bringelkoopf, I haven't seen signs of any others."

"Those that did not return to their home worlds remained on Portalia, but different species settled on different continents. As part of the conditions of Stewardship, humans agreed to remain on this continent, and not venture beyond."

Sammy jumped on that. "Didn't you, like, just give us the whole 'humanity must explore or die' lecture? Now you're saying humans have never left this continent?"

Michael chuckled. "Yes, it's true. Humans need to explore. But Portalians have focused their passions on internal exploration. Portalians are very connected to Portalia, in a way that Earth humans are not connected to Earth. They express themselves through a myriad of beautiful art, food, and storytelling."

"Music is an internal art," Sammy said. "Grolfshin has been seeking kids with musical talent. If Portalians are so focused on art, why don't more have musical ability?"

"Because the Great Shutters made sure that those with innate musical ability were not amongst the humans selected to remain on Portalia. Otherwise, they may not have been as successful in keeping humans contained for as long as they have. As I said, many believe it was an unforgivable act."

"But couldn't the humans on Earth just use their ability to port back like I did?" I asked. "Portalia is unique in her ability to connect. New portals can only be built on Portalia. To come to Portalia from Earth requires the use of an existing port. And the locations of those were a closely guarded secret. That is how the humans on Earth were kept shut out."

Michael's eyes flitted to me. "Like Earthlings, Portalians have grown restless from being so long contained. And now, Grolfshin has decided not to honor the agreement to remain on this continent."

"Why?" I asked

"I'm not sure."

"Because he's an imbecile," Bringelkoopf said.

"So those other species, they're all stuck here?" Sammy asked.

"They had their choices, Sammy, each of them. Some liked it here and wanted to stay. Others, like the unicorns and dragons, stayed to follow their own destinies."

Sammy snorted. "Unicorns and dragons are myths."

"Many myths have their origins in reality. Unicorns and dragons no longer exist on Earth, but I assure you they do exist on Portalia."

Sammy refused to be duped. "Okay. Show me one."

Michael chortled. "They aren't particularly fond of humans."

"Can't imagine why that would be," Bringelkoopf said.

"Seriously?" Sammy's voice held a mixture of hope and skepticism. "There really are dragons and unicorns?"

"Do you think I would lie to you?"

Sammy thought about that for a moment, then his face exploded with a delighted grin. "Wow. That's very, very cool."

I didn't have the heart to remind him that Michael had lied through his teeth about the taste of the green sludge he'd pawned off on Teleana.

"What do you mean, they stayed to follow their destinies?" I asked.

"I must be honest. I know little of the dragons' destiny. They are a very reclusive and exceptionally temperamental species. I've not seen one in ten years."

"And even that hasn't been long enough," Bringelkoopf said.

"As for the unicorns," Michael continued, "they are the keepers of the portal maps. They cannot open or create portals. But they have the ability to locate and shut any existing port. To answer your earlier question, Jacob, the unicorns are the ones who shut the ports at Giza and Stonehenge.

"Like humans, the destinies of the dragons and the unicorns are entwined. Unicorns and dragons are dedicated to honor and destiny. Even though humans have treated them poorly, they will not shirk their duty due to their dislike of humans."

"Were you and Bringelkoopf stranded here too?" Sammy asked.

"We both came here by choice. Our worlds do have extremely limited access to Portalia, but those ports are not on this continent."

"Then why are you here?" I asked.

"I am from Eliosha. Teaching is our birthright. My people worried that the Great Shutting would cause irreparable damage to humanity's soul. So we offered ourselves as Teachers. We agreed not to interfere, but to support and teach, in order that humanity could reclaim its destiny.

"In exchange, we extracted an agreement that never again would the Great Shutters interfere with another species' free will in the course of the fulfillment of its destiny. In short, Jacob, I am your Teacher. As I was your father's and his before him."

"How long have you been here?" I asked.

Sadness tinged Michael's voice. "I've not been home for five hundred fifty years."

Sammy and I dropped our jaws in unison. It was beyond our ability to comprehend.

After a very, very long silence I asked, "Don't you miss your family?"

"The place where we are born is our birthplace. The place where we follow our chosen path in life is our home. Portalia is my home. This is the destiny I have chosen."

"Are you from Eliosha too?" I asked Bringelkoopf.

"Absolutely not. I told you I am Koopf."

"But where are you from?"

"Um, I'm from Koopf. What part of 'Koopf' are you not hearing?"

"I thought you said—" I caught Michael's laughing eyes, and realized I would get nowhere with the not-a-ferret. "So, why are you here then? Are you a Teacher too?"

Bringelkoopf literally fell over laughing and even Michael shook with barely contained mirth. When Michael determined I'd suffered enough, he said, "Answer his question, my friend."

"Actually, originally I came to spy on humans."

"You're a spy?" Sammy shrieked.

"No, of course not, I mean, I was, but I...." Bringelkoopf drummed his teeth with his claws, and I was certain the not-a-ferret was blushing scarlet red beneath his fur.

"Yes?" Sammy prompted, quite obviously enjoying Bringelkoopf's sudden discomfort.

"Well, I, um, I sort of, um...." He looked to Michael for help but Michael shook his head to tell him he was on his own.

Bringelkoopf sighed. "I met Michael and he showed me a different side of humans. Indeed, I find them to be interesting and eccentric creatures. So when it came time for me to return to Koopf and give my report, well, I just didn't." He turned and snapped at Michael. "At this rate, he'll die of old age before you finish."

"Thank you, my friend." Michael's eyes twinkled with amusement.

The carving was taking shape. It looked like a heart. But, as with all things with Michael, it was not that simple.

"I never understood why the unicorns told him." Michael caught me off guard with the sudden shift back to unicorns. "They'd not involved themselves in human affairs for centuries. But now I know...."

Suddenly, Michael spoke to me as if I were the only person in all the universe. "Jacob, it hasn't been easy for me to guide and support those I love, without interfering, without forsaking my oath. I loved your father and Grolfshin both very much, Jacob. I still do."

A glittering teardrop fell from his eye and soaked into his carving, unnoticed by everyone, it seemed, but me. "I remember them as little boys. Grolfshin worshipped your father. He trundled after him wherever he went. They were the closest of friends."

"So what happened?"

"Grolfshin became close with the Vorkalis family. He changed. Your father didn't want to see it at first. Even when he did, he never lost hope. He insisted that, if he had enough time, he could love Grolfshin better."

Michael had stopped whittling, his hands so heavy with sadness that they no longer moved.

"Your father didn't think Guardians were any better, or worse, than non-Guardians. But Grolfshin, ever since he was little, liked the idea that he was born better than others. Prantos humored him. He said it was nothing more than a slightly annoying character flaw."

"Is that why he was so peeved that he was nursed by a non-Guardian?" Sammy asked.

Michael nodded. "He blames any weakness of his on that poor woman."

"Sounds like Grolfie had more than a 'slightly annoying character flaw,'" Sammy said.

Bringelkoopf snickered.

Michael's eyes begged me for forgiveness. "I know you must be angry with me, Jacob, for not telling you more. Please understand, I couldn't say or do anything that would have interfered with your ability to choose your own path, your own destiny."

I held my breath as he continued, for I knew another bombshell was about to be dropped.

"The unicorns knew it all along," he whispered, peering at me with a bright intensity that raised the hackles on the back of my neck.

"The unicorns showed your father the very last port to Earth — the portal in your clubhouse. It had been hidden from humans since before the Great Shutting. And the unicorns showed it to your father. After you were born. After they'd sworn him to secrecy, even from his brother.

"I thought it was your father the unicorns were interested in, but it wasn't, it never was. "It was you, Jacob. It was always you. And the unicorns knew it."

LEGEND OF THE UNICORNS

"THE LEGEND OF the Unicorns was written thousands of years ago and has been passed down through the Prios family for every generation since," Michael continued.

"I should have known, even before the unicorns took an interest in you," Michael said again, as if it hadn't been enough of a shock the first time. "But I thought...." His eyes flickered briefly to the hall door, then he laughed as if he had just found what he'd been looking for and it had been in front of his nose all along.

Michael resumed whittling, his hands moving like the wings of a hummingbird, which appear not to be moving at all but are actually moving too fast for the eye to see.

He began to chant, and as he chanted, I was slammed back in time with a force more intense than the shock wave that had knocked me over when I closed the port from the dungeon. My father's voice roared into my head as clearly as if he were speaking directly into my ear.

Then, just as abruptly, his voice was washed away and replaced by Michael's voice. Not Michael's voice in the present, but Michael's voice from a time so very, very long ago.

* * *

This wasn't a memory of Little Me. It was a memory of Baby Me.

Baby Me snuggled into the crook of a warm, comforting, cinnamon and apple smelling elbow and gazed into sparkling, twinkling eyes.

"Okay, my sweet Jacob," the man said, "once more, but then it really is bedtime."

Baby Me listened happily as the man chanted his favorite tale:

> In Portalia's garden, Earth's children once played in harmony
> Never suspecting Portalia held the key to their ultimate destiny
> For in her garden Portalia holds many a secret door
> Through which life will one day spread its wings and soar
> Young humans, when they discovered these doors, were difficult to contain
> In their youthful eagerness, they inflicted much pain
> It was decided, humanity needed time to grow and mature
> So a period of seclusion, Portalians would need to endure
> After a time of darkness, and separation from her sister Earth
> A son of Portalia will return to the place of his father's birth
> His soul will sing a song of harmony Portalia will hear
> Causing her portals to fling open, and new ones to appear
> His gates Portalia need not shut to protect against disaster
> For he is her guardian and protector, he is the portal master
> Like Portalia, he is humble, for power he does not seek
> He will stand in defense of all, be they mighty or meek
> His heart will be pure, full of love, with no malice, greed or hate
> His compassion will lift the burden of pain and sorrow's heavy weight
> Once and forever, many worlds he will reunite
> So that all peoples may pursue their destinies, and to the stars take flight
> Upon his arrival, Portalia will rejoice and sing
> For he is her guardian, the portal master, and most of all, her people's King

* * *

Michael's voice faded and reluctantly I drew myself back from the memory of the cozy haven of his arms. I tried to swallow, but my mouth was so dry that my tongue stuck to its roof.

Sammy cocked his head to the side. "You think Jacob's the guy in the unicorn legend?"

Michael nodded. "For centuries, it was rare to have anyone with porting ability. But over the last century, there has been a Prios in every generation with the ability. And not just Prioses."

That surprised me. "You mean others too?"

"None with more than a weak ability. But the ability has been growing stronger. It's as though Portalia knows that the time to fulfill the Legend has come. And it was always thought that the one who fulfilled the Legend would be born during Portal Week. Your grandfather, King Talarcos, was born during Portal Week."

Michael chuckled in fond remembrance. "Talarcos was an ornery child, but he was a good man and his gift was strong. When the unicorn Petros befriended him, we thought he might be the one.

"But Petros was just as much a loveable rebel as your grandfather, and their friendship, well, it had nothing to do with the Legend. Then your father was born, also during Portal Week, and I was very sure he was the one. Even as a young boy he had a regal presence and a pure heart. I knew he'd do great things."

Michael softened as he spoke of my father. He always does. "When the unicorn Piltan befriended him, I was certain that meant something."

My world was spinning so fast that I almost missed it. Piltan. I'd heard that name before. Bringelkoopf had mentioned him in the dungeon. Piltan was my father's friend. And, it seems, he was also a unicorn.

"I think it was a case of wanting it to be true," Michael went on. "Because we've been waiting for so very long. However, your father's talent, though strong, was not strong enough."

Michael's eyes again flickered involuntarily towards the hall door. "You, too, were born during Portal Week, and...." He stopped, overwhelmed with emotion and unable to continue.

Sammy narrowed his eyes. I could almost see the synapses in his brain firing rapidly. "You thought it would be Teleana's child." He spoke so softly I was sure I'd misheard him. "That's why Grolfshin captured her."

"I don't understand," I said.

"Jacob," Sammy said. "Teleana's your sister."

I waited for Michael to tell Sammy he was wrong. Only he didn't.

"She looks a lot like you, Jacob," Sammy explained, as if it was so obvious he couldn't believe he hadn't figured it out sooner.

"But...but...I don't understand." My fingers scrambled for something to tweak and roll, and settled on a chunk of bread. Not the best idea. Bread tends to crumble under such an assault.

Michael spoke with that gentleness one uses with frightened animals and cowering puppies. "Your father fell in love with a girl named Liliana when he was young. But she was not a Guardian and Portalians expect their King to marry a Guardian.

"He wanted to abdicate the throne. But she felt your father had an important destiny, so she broke off with him and married his close friend, Pierce Parston. Liliana was pregnant with Teleana at the time. I don't know if she intended to tell your father, but she died giving birth. And Pierce chose to raise Teleana as his own."

I was floored. I had a sister. And I'd just rescued my sister and her unborn child from the dungeon where our uncle had imprisoned us.

"Does she know?" I asked.

"Yes, she figured it out years ago."

"And Milokah?"

Michael scratched Bringelkoopf. "He knows. They are not related, but they are siblings."

Michael continued in his gentle, puppy-comforting voice. "I know now that Teleana's child is not the fulfillment of the Legend. I should have known, but even I am not perfect."

"Hmmpf. I could have told you that," Bringelkoopf said.

"What makes you so sure I'm the one? You could be wrong, right? I mean, maybe you were right about Teleana? Maybe my destiny was to protect her baby?" I rambled like a drowning man reaches at ocean foam in hopes that the bubbly froth will somehow turn out to be a lifesaver. But I already knew the truth.

Michael brushed bits of microscopic dust from his woodwork and blew gently across its surface. He tilted it side to side and inspected it closely, flicking the tip of his blade expertly, just so, here, and there. All the while avoiding my frantic eyes.

"For thousands of years, humans have taught themselves not to listen to their souls, Jacob. But not you. You believe your soul, you listen to it, and you refuse to give up on your dreams. Because of that, your soul's music is pure."

Michael spoke with a forceful passion that I could not have ignored if I tried, which I did.

"Jacob, my people delight in the privilege and honor of being educators. Education has allowed countless species to feed and nourish their souls and thereby help them on their journeys. You cannot possibly imagine the depth of my agony, to see what humans have done with the very thing my people value so highly.

"Instead of allowing education to help them in the quest for exploration and discovery that fuels their passion and feeds their souls, they have used it to completely silence their souls. Until I met my first human, I would not have believed it possible. And it is killing them."

For a moment, I thought Michael had gotten sidetracked. He hadn't.

His eyes seared into me. "Every person has the right to make his or her own choices in life, Jacob. You, too, are free to choose. You, and only you, can choose your destiny."

Bringelkoopf stretched up and rubbed his head against Michael's knuckles. "Jacob," he said quietly, "that port you opened from the dungeon?"

"Yeah?" I wanted nothing more than to crawl to safety under the table.

"You built a new port, Jacob," he said. "You built a port where one did not exist."

"So?" I'd had to get Milokah and Sammy and Teleana to safety. I'd had to.

"Jacob," Michael said, "there has not been a new port built since before the Great Shutting. In three thousand years, many have tried, but none have succeeded. Until now. Until *you*."

The magnitude of what Michael had just said was not lost on Sammy. His mug actually slipped from his grasp and fell into his lap.

Sammy and I looked at each other. I suspected my face was as colorless as his. I knew what he was thinking. He was thinking the same thing I was thinking.

You'd think that finding out that you were the fulfillment of an ages-old legend, one that just happened to have been written by unicorns, and that you'd just accomplished something nobody else had been able to for thousands of years, would be cool. But you'd be wrong. It was not cool, it was scary. Even Sammy got that.

Michael lifted his glowing eyes to mine and his voice trembled when he spoke.

"Jacob, I have waited my entire life to serve you. You are Portalia's guardian, her portal master, and her people's King. That is your destiny, if you choose to accept it."

A FAMILY OF FRIENDS

VISIONS ROARED THROUGH my head like tidal waves. Along with a voice, my father's voice, telling me story after story. Of unicorns and eagles. Of exotic lands and peoples. Of legends and destinies.

Tales so vivid I couldn't believe I'd never before remembered any of them. I found myself yearning for the orange-and-red rock in my clubhouse, with the sudden certainty that I would soon need it, though I didn't know why.

My father hadn't just gifted me with a super-cool kids' hangout and an orange-and-red rock. He'd gifted me with a destiny and a duty. He hadn't built me a clubhouse at all, he'd built me a vault. A place to keep safe all the precious secrets and memories which now flooded me. A place from which I could one day connect with him, reclaim our heritage, and set sail on my destiny.

I clutched my head to try to quiet the torrent.

Sammy tapped my shoulder. "Jakey?"

"I'm okay."

"You sure?"

I nodded, as if by nodding I could make it true.

I hadn't grown into my ears yet. I wasn't ready to be the person everybody thought I was. I'd barely had the guts to apologize to Milokah within earshot of Sammy.

Then my father spoke, as he had a few hours ago, from deep within me. "You *are* that person, my son. You *have* to be. These are your people. This is your destiny."

My fingers dove into my pockets and settled into a plucking and tweaking tempo that matched the drumbeat of my heart.

Slowly, the roaring subsided, and I was able to lift my head enough to look around the table.

Bringelkoopf still crouched by his shavings pile. Sammy remained perched on the bench beside me. Michael's hands still worked their magic with the knife. Nothing had changed in the last five minutes. Except my entire world.

"It's just, you know, a lot to take in," I said. Perhaps I could simply sit here forever and watch bits of wood fall victim to Bringelkoopf. That sounded relaxing.

My fingers delighted in a tuft of fabric they'd newly freed from my forlorn pocket.

"You'll be fine, you know," Bringelkoopf said.

"Uh huh." My head bobbed up and down, but not so much that my eyes lost their grip on the woodcarving show. It had to be an angel. I was sure of it.

"Hey, I got a question," Sammy said.

"Yes, Sammy?" Michael said.

"If Teleana is Jacob's older sister, why isn't she the heir to the throne?"

Yes. Of course. Teleana was my father's first child. *She* should be the heir. That would relieve me of being everyone's hope.

Like many of my hopes, it was short-lived.

"Her mother was never married to Prantos, so Teleana is not eligible to inherit the throne," Michael said.

"That's stupid," I said.

"Yeah," Sammy agreed. "That's like something out of the Dark Ages."

Michael chuckled. "Yes, Sammy, but you must remember, Portalia is, in many ways, like your Dark Ages. And the laws about royal lineage were established long ago."

"It's still stupid," Sammy insisted.

Michael gestured at me with his knife. "I am optimistic that Jacob intends to rewrite the laws of ascension. I imagine he will change that part, in particular."

"What are laws of ascension and why do you think I'll want to rewrite them?"

Michael's eyes held a mischievous glint. "You are King because you are your father's son. Born of his wedded wife."

"So?" I probably would have caught on sooner, but my mind was still spinning.

Michael nodded at the door to the hallway. "Milokah cannot give you heirs. Unless you change the laws of ascension, you will either have to abdicate your children's rights to their heritage, or marry a woman and be untrue to yourself and the one you love."

Denial leapt onto the tip of my tongue. But I fought it. I wouldn't deny Milokah again, not even for Sammy. I held my breath and waited for Sammy to register Michael's words.

"Why do you say Milokah?" Sammy asked. "They only just met. Isn't it a little early to be planning their wedding? Or do they really get married that young on Portalia?"

"Prios men are notorious for knowing their hearts, and falling in love, at a very young age. Jacob's grandfather, Talarcos, declared his love at seven, and his great-grandfather, Jaconiah, at eight. I say Milokah because I know the look of love on a Prios man's face. But though they tend to know quite young who they intend to marry, they do not marry until they've reached the age of maturity."

Sammy pondered that for about two seconds before he moved on to his next question. "Can two guys get married on Portalia?"

"Of course."

Sammy snorted. "Seems kinda weird, don't you think?"

"Why would it be weird Sammy?" Michael asked, bemused.

"Well, two guys can marry, which is totally cool, but Teleana's out of the running for the throne because her parents weren't married? I would have thought if Portalians were enlightened about same-sex marriage, they'd be enlightened about lines of ascension as well."

"Humans are a peculiar species, Sammy."

"You can say that again." Sammy emphasized the point by tearing off another chunk of bread.

"Marriage is a matter of love," Michael went on. "Laws of royal ascension are a matter of law. Sometimes, the law forgets to take matters of love into consideration."

I stared at Sammy and Michael in shock. They were carrying on a whole conversation about me being in love with Milokah and marrying him someday, like I wasn't even in the room. And Sammy wasn't freaked out or disgusted, he was just his usual curious self.

I'd worked so hard to hide what I was from Sammy. Yet he hadn't even batted an eye.

Sammy laughed and swatted my shoulder. "Dude, I call dibs on being best man."

But when he saw the look on my face, his laugh faltered. "What?"

"You...you..."

"I what?"

"I think Jacob is shocked that you're not shocked," Michael said.

"About what? I thought you liked Milokah. He seems like a nice guy."

"I do. But you said gay guys disgusted you and gave you the creeps."

"When did I ever say that?"

"When Marcus Calvin was holding hands with his boyfriend at Mike's. You said—"

"I know what I said," Sammy snapped. He looked angry. And hurt, like Milokah had.

"Marcus is a disgusting creep." Sammy wiped his face brusquely. "He was my mom's dealer. He and his buddies would hang out at my house for days, stoned and wasted and playing mean tricks on me and making me try stuff because they thought it was funny."

I knew hardly anything about Sammy's home. I'd asked a few times, but it made him so miserable that I'd stopped.

"But today, when you saw me with Milokah, in the meadow, you had a funny look."

"You looked happy, until you looked up at me," Sammy said, sounding even more hurt. "Then you looked scared. And for a second, I thought you were scared of him. Then I realized that you were scared of *me*."

"You mean, you knew? All day long, you've known?"

"All day long? Jakey, I've always known. I just didn't care." He wiped a fresh batch of tears from his face. It was the second time in two days I'd made my best friend cry.

"How many times have I told you I love you just the way you are?" he asked.

"Yeah, but I thought that was because you didn't know."

"How could you think that of me? You were the one who couldn't accept it, Jakey, not me. You were the one who wanted to believe it wasn't true, not me. You were the one who hid from it."

He looked like I'd betrayed him. And, I realized, that's exactly what I had done.

I'd as much as told him he was just like Jimmy. I was the worst friend. Ever.

"I'm sorry," I whispered. "I'm sorry." That made two people I'd hurt because I was trying to protect myself.

Sammy wiped his face with his shirt. "I forgive you. And I'm glad you found Milokah. I like him. When I saw you two together, you had a smile on your face that I've never seen before. It was good, Jakey, really good. A happy smile, you know?"

"Yeah, I do."

"But it wasn't right, what you did to him."

"I know."

"You're lucky he forgave you. You can't play with people's hearts that way."

"I know." I looked at the door and wondered how soon Milokah would come back. I needed to show him that I wasn't going to deny him, not ever again.

It had been for nothing. All that time. Sammy knew. He just didn't care.

A heavy swoosh from the entryway interrupted my musings. A fireball of motherly energy descended into the room.

"Where is she?" Ma Korsen boomed.

Two things were immediately clear. First, her name was most definitely Ma, whether or not she had any children of her own. Second, I would never, ever be tempted to call her "This Ma Person."

It wasn't that she was scary. Quite the opposite. Ma Korsen looked like she belonged on the cover of a cookbook. Not an exotic cookbook, but an oh-so-delicious, full-of-butter-and-sugar-cookie cookbook. She was even wearing an apron with suspicious smudges on the front. I wouldn't have been surprised to see her march to the hearth and pull out an apple pie.

Except that instead of going to the hearth, she marched straight to me, clasped my cheeks between her flour-smudged hands, and planted a kiss on my nose.

"Thought you'd forgotten all about us, young man." She took one look at my face and hugged me so tight I couldn't breathe. "There, there, my love, everything's going to be alright. Don't you worry."

"And who's this?" she asked, floating to Sammy. Before Sammy could answer, she put him through the same cheek-grabbing, kiss-planting, rib-crushing hug.

When she let go, Sammy gasped, "Hi, I'm...Sammy."

But Ma was on a mission, and didn't wait to hear his response. She buzzed to the hearth, where she did not magically produce an apple pie, but did slow down just long enough to snatch a chunk of bread, swish it in the pot, and toss it in her mouth.

"Perfect as always, Mr. Michael," she said.

I could have sworn I saw the hall door cringe in anticipation of impending discomfort as Ma Korsen bulldozed through the last obstacle standing between her and her Teleana.

She was gone in a flash and the door swung itself shut with a quiver.

The breath of warmth that Ma had brought with her was shattered by Mr. Korsen. Whereas Ma's entry had been like a whirlwind, his was as painfully slow as molasses. And there was nothing apple-pie-cozy about Mr. Korsen.

He emanated all the warmth of a hungry grizzly bear. And he was glaring fiercely at me as he lumbered ever so slowly toward us.

"Hello, Breskin," Michael said. "Why don't you have a seat?"

Mr. Korsen lowered himself beside Michael, looking for all the world like a very unhappy two-year-old. A huge, beefy, intimidating two-year-old.

"Jacob, this is Mr. Korsen. He is Teleana's uncle, on her mother's side," Michael said.

"Nice to meet you, Sir," I said.

Mr. Korsen folded his arms and scowled.

Michael maneuvered Mr. Korsen with the deftness one might expect of someone who has likely smoothed many ruffled feathers and patched up quite a few wounded egos over the last several hundred years.

"Breskin, I have just been telling Jacob all about Portalia. He was not even four when his father passed. And until this day, he has not known any of our history. Poor lad, it's quite a lot to take in, as you can well imagine."

Michael threw an arm around Mr. Korsen's shoulders, as one ally to another. "I know you and Prantos were very close, Breskin."

Mr. Korsen grunted, but his shoulders softened fractionally.

Michael continued, "I am sure, before he died, that Prantos took solace in knowing that when Jacob returned you would be someone upon whom he could rely and trust."

"Yes, I'm sure he did." Mr. Korsen spoke as if the words were being pulled from him.

Michael smiled and squeezed Mr. Korsen's shoulder. Then, as if they had been talking of nothing more than the weather, he resumed the smooth glide and flick of his blade.

"And who are you?" Mr. Korsen grumbled at Sammy.

Sammy shoved a piece of bread to the side of his mouth. "Sammy. Nice to meet you."

"Hmmpf."

After that, we sat in one of those horribly awkward silences. Well, almost silence. Michael hummed, but it wasn't enough to break through the tension.

I thought about nudging Bringelkoopf to see if he would say something sarcastic to lighten the mood. My toe inched itself toward the blissfully unaware not-a-ferret. Fortunately for all of us, Milokah burst into the room and stopped my eager toe in its tracks.

"Ma wants more of the green stuff," he said.

When Mr. Korsen saw Milokah, he morphed almost instantly into a cuddly, overgrown teddy bear. He still reminded me of a two-year-old, only now he looked like a two-year-old eagerly reaching out for a hug from his favorite person.

"Milo, how are you? How's Telly?"

"She's fine." Milokah flung his arms around Mr. Korsen. "Ma says it should be soon."

"Really? She's okay?" I asked.

Milokah laughed. "Yes, Jacob, she's okay. Don't worry. Ma's delivered lots of babies."

He ran his fingers through his thick black hair and gave me the universe's brightest and most perfect smile. I could easily believe that he'd forgotten everyone else in the room existed. Like I had.

Milokah looked back and forth between me and Sammy. When he saw the goofy way I grinned at him, even in front of Sammy, happiness flooded him and he returned the goofy grin.

My heart danced with joy and even Mr. Korsen's scowl could not dampen my spirits.

Then Milokah hopped up and snatched the bottle of green stuff. "I'll let you know when something changes." He disappeared through the door almost as quickly as Ma had.

His smile had given me a boost of strength.

"Mr. Korsen, you don't seem too thrilled to see me."

"Your father was my King. And my friend. And he abandoned us."

"He didn't abandon you. He died to protect Portalia."

Sammy looked at me in surprise. At first I thought he was surprised to hear me standing up for my father. Then I realized that I hadn't told him about the memory of how my father died.

Mr. Korsen shook his head. "All men have choices, even Kings."

His words made my skin tingle. He sounded eerily like Rick had just two days ago.

A deep, long lingering pain poked through Mr. Korsen's anger. "When I see what has become of my beloved Portalia, when I think of what the Prios family, and Grolfshin, have done to us, when I think of my dear...." He choked, unable to continue.

But I knew what he was going to say. Teleana. My sister. My father's first child.

As if reading my thoughts, Mr. Korsen continued. "Don't misunderstand me. Pierce Parston is her father through and through. I would strike down any man who suggested otherwise. But your father made choices that hurt many people."

"I am not my father, Mr. Korsen. What have I done?"

"Nothing," he spat. "That's just it, you've done nothing. You are going to have to prove yourself to many people, Jacob, before you can earn their trust, their loyalty, and their respect."

"I know." He'd used my first name. It was a start. And he was right. My people had suffered greatly, so they would not be quick to trust. I would need to prove myself.

Michael coughed. "Breskin, there is something you should know."

Mr. Korsen raised a cautious eyebrow. "Yes?"

"It is him," Michael said. "He is the one."

For a minute, Mr. Korsen appeared not to know what Michael was talking about. I watched the transformation on his face as the realization gradually hit home.

He snorted, and, like Michael had earlier, looked longingly at the hall door. Behind it my sister was about to give birth to her baby. The baby he, like many, had thought would be the one.

Suddenly, we were all startled by a loud, persistent thumping from the entryway. Someone was knocking on Michael's front door.

From the very worried looks Michael and Mr. Korsen exchanged, it was clear that whoever was knocking had not been invited.

"Wait here," Michael said.

While Michael went to see who it was, Mr. Korsen planted himself in front of the door.

I fought a surge of hysterical laughter. After all that had happened, had I failed to protect my sister's baby from being raised in a dungeon after all?

Was this to be my father's legacy? That I had discovered my destiny too late? That I'd discovered my family and my roots just in time to fail them and lose them all forever?

A DANGER TOO GREAT

BEVERLY, MY UNCLE'S GIRLFRIEND. That's who Michael had his arm wrapped around when he returned with our unexpected visitor.

Mr. Korsen immediately brought himself down from high-alert status.

But even though no one with creepy yellow eyes followed them in, Sammy and I were still confused as Michael escorted Beverly to the table.

"Here, dear," he said, rubbing her arm, "come have a seat. I'll get you some stew."

Beverly sat numbly. Mr. Korsen clapped a comforting paw on her arm.

A mug of stew, with typical Michael flourish, appeared magically in front of her. Beverly gripped it so tightly that her fingers turned white. "It's bad, worse than ever." She darted her eyes nervously at me. "I've never seen him this way before."

Mr. Korsen snorted.

"No, it's true, Breskin. Losing them both...." She stopped and glanced about frantically. "Oh my, where is Teleana?"

Michael patted her hand. "She's fine. Ma is with her."

Reassured, Beverly continued. "He told me some things he never has before, and he showed me this." Her hands shook as she withdrew a frayed bit of yellow parchment and handed it, with great trepidation, to Michael.

Michael smoothed out the parchment and his eyes narrowed as he scanned it.

"Harold is furious that Grolfshin lost both Teleana and Jacob," Beverly said. "Grolfshin's put out a reward for them and he has the forests crawling with men and dogs."

Mr. Korsen slammed his fist on the table. "That evil, miserable... I should snap his neck."

"This isn't him, Breskin," Beverly said. "It's Harold. Can't you see, it's not him."

"She's right. It's not his fault." I looked to see who'd spoken. Then I realized it was me.

Beverly looked at me as if she'd stepped into a bizarre alternate reality. One in which there really was someone who might not completely hate the man she loved.

Sammy gawked at me like I had horns growing out of my head. "Not his *fault*? Are you out of your mind?"

"Probably," said Bringelkoopf.

"He's hurting," I said. "He thought my dad had left him."

"So what? *My* dad left me. *Your* dad died. We didn't turn into bullies or tyrants."

My brain agreed, but my heart took sides against me. I repeated what Milokah had said, seemingly so very long ago, but in reality only just earlier today. "When people are hurt, some turn that pain into love and some turn it into hate. It's easier to hate than to love."

"That doesn't make it right, Jakey."

"I know that."

Michael pushed the parchment to the side. There were no sparkles in his eyes, no twinkles, no swirls. And when he spoke, it was with an eerie calmness, as though telling the punch line to a sickening joke. "When King Prantos the Second banished the Helxin family after Stonehenge, it seems he felt banishment was an excessively harsh punishment for such a murderous lot. So he left this letter, with the location of the port, and asked that the family be allowed to rejoin Portalia someday."

Michael stroked the edges of the parchment. His calmness evaporated and small, dark swirls formed in his eyes. "These directions lead to the very same port that King Jacob the First used to banish the werewolves from Giza, three thousand years ago."

"I thought you said that he had the unicorns shut that port," Sammy said.

Michael's neck veins bulged like garden hoses. "It is painfully obvious that he did not. The werewolves were dangerous. Evil. Powerful. Why did I not see this?"

"See what?" I asked.

"They had yellow eyes. They had a hypnotic power." Michael's body shook with so much rage that he looked like he might explode. "They could turn a mother against her son," he paused, then added with a soft, spiteful laugh, "they could turn a King against his own people."

"So, what you're saying," Sammy said, "is that Harold may be descended from a family made up of evil, hypnotic werewolves and the murderous Helxins?"

Sammy has always been great at taking long, drawn-out stories and summarizing them into concise snapshots. Usually, I appreciated that particular skill of his. This time I did not.

"Yes," Michael said. "And King Talarcos brought them back to Portalia, settled them quietly in the county of Vorkalis and gave them a dukedom and an official claim to the royal throne."

His words made me think of my horrible nightmare.

"I keep having this dream. There's a cowering purple puppy, and a black wolf with a red beard and yellow eyes is towering menacingly over him."

"Michael?" Beverly looked miserable, like her bad news was far from over. "He says that Harold has a device that can keep a port open."

Absentmindedly, I wrapped my fingers around the forgotten lump of ivory I'd found on Freedom's planet after escaping the dungeon.

Beverly went on. "It's not possible, is it? Harold's brother Felix had one. He went to Earth. But he never came back. If it worked, he would have come back, right?"

At her words, an excruciating acid-like pain radiated outwards from my heart as I remembered the very last time I'd seen my father. My fingers rubbed the piece of ivory so vigorously that they started to go numb.

"I was four," I whispered. "He came to the clubhouse. He had a funny rope in his hand. My dad called him Felix. He had yellow eyes. And a red beard. Rocco tried to get to him but he couldn't because my dad had finally put the new latch on the screen door like Mom had asked. He took Felix in the car with him. Then a policeman came and told us they were both dead."

I flung the chunk of ivory onto the table as if it were the cause of the burning pain in my chest. "I think he knew what that rope was, and he died to make sure Felix couldn't use it."

Michael stared at the ivory and his eyes began to change, but I didn't notice at first. In fact, none of us did. We were all equally oblivious to Michael as I went on.

"In the dungeon, Harold wrapped a rope just like it around my leg. It hurt so bad, I thought my foot would be cut off. I kept trying to close the port, but it wouldn't close."

"What is it?" Sammy asked.

"Grolfshin told me it's made from the horn and tail of unicorns," Beverly said.

That's when we finally noticed Michael's eyes. I'd seen the pinpoints of light within his eyes twinkle with grandfatherly coziness. I'd seen them swirl with dull, dark anger. I'd seen them sparkle explosively with excitement.

Yes, I'd seen Michael's glittering eyes do all sorts of things and I'd gotten so used to the strange things his eyes did that I'd almost forgotten that, in general, people's eyes did not do those sorts of things.

But now Michael's eyes were doing something very different and much scarier. They were smoldering and smoking with dark vortices of seething rage. They did not look even vaguely, remotely, like Michael's eyes.

In fact, I realized with a sickening pit in my stomach, Michael did not look like Michael.

Not only had those wonderful, twinkling eyes disappeared, but also my Michael—my warm, safe, grandfatherly Michael—had disappeared.

He hadn't changed physically in the way that transformers morph from one thing to another, but he'd transformed all the same. He loomed so tall that he should not have been able to fit within his cabin. His shoulders swelled and his body tensed as if he was readying for battle. A battle which there was no doubt he would win.

My breath caught in my throat. It was the very first time I'd looked at Michael and not had any difficulty believing that he wasn't human. I wasn't the only one.

Sammy dropped his bread. Mr. Korsen licked his lips nervously. Beverly wrung her hands. And Bringelkoopf stopped tormenting his precious wood shavings.

In unison we stared with dread at the complete stranger sitting at our table. None of us existed for Michael. All that existed for Michael was the chunk of unicorn horn on the table.

The air in Michael's cabin became charged with a cold, static electricity that caused the hair on my arms to stand up, my heart to shudder, and my skin to tingle. Were it not for the smell of cinnamon, apples and something else that still wafted over to me from the hearth, it would have been easy to forget that Michael's cabin had ever felt like a cozy, safe haven.

It was Bringelkoopf who finally found the courage to move. The not-a-ferret crept cautiously, fearfully and very, very bravely onto the table, towards Michael.

But Michael did not see his closest and dearest friend as the vortices in his eyes spun violently, releasing horrible dark puffs of billowing smoke. Nor did he see his furry companion as his fingers wrapped themselves around the parchment and squeezed.

Bringelkoopf nudged Michael's hand. "Michael," he said tentatively.

There was no response.

Bringelkoopf nudged his hand again, this time more forcefully. Still nothing.

Then he boomed in a voice so deep that I could not believe it came from him, "Michael!"

But Michael was gone, deeply withdrawn into his internal inferno.

Bringelkoopf picked up the piece of unicorn horn. "I'm sorry. I'm so sorry."

At first I thought he was apologizing to us because he couldn't bring Michael back from his dark place. Then I realized he was apologizing to Michael for what he was about to do.

He hurled the piece of unicorn horn violently across the cabin. As it ricocheted off the wall he sank his fangs savagely into Michael's hand. My ear throbbed in sympathy.

Michael's eyes barely flickered and he did not budge. Once more, Bringelkoopf buried his fangs into Michael's white-knuckled fist. Still Michael did not return to us.

With tears streaming down his face, Bringelkoopf clambered up Michael's arm, cemented himself to Michael's ear, and chanted frantically in a strange language.

For several tense minutes, it felt hopeless. Then there was a faint decrease in the cold electric charge of the air in the cabin.

Ever so gradually, Michael's death grip relaxed, his hand fell open and the crumbled dust that had been the parchment flowed from his palm.

His battle-ready shoulders deflated and a warm coziness began to filter back into the room. Ever so slowly, Michael's body ceased to look like a warrior. It began to look like it could possibly belong to someone trying to appear like a human grandfather.

Not until a faint sparkle replaced the smoldering in his eyes did I allow my shoulders to relax. When his lips cracked into a reassuring smile, we all knew that it was forced but it comforted us even so. Though he was still in pain, Michael was back.

Bringelkoopf retrieved the unicorn horn and placed it gently on the table. "I'm sorry," he whispered.

Michael stroked his fur gently with the hand that moments earlier had pulverized a piece of parchment. "I know, my friend, I know."

Michael swallowed. "Talarcos's unicorn friend Petros once told me that the power to hold open a gate exists within unicorns. Petros disappeared after Talarcos died. I always thought he'd returned to Unicorn Isle without saying good bye. But this is him. I can feel it."

"That's his horn?" Sammy asked. "You mean they just chopped it off him?"

"It is impossible to remove the horn from a unicorn while he is alive, Sammy."

Sammy bit back a strangled sob as he realized what that meant.

"Oh, Talarcos, what have you done?" Michael hissed with such anger and pain that I wished I could rip out my heart so I couldn't feel it.

"If Harold can control minds, and he has a device to keep ports open, what happens if he finds Jacob?" Sammy asked.

In a dazed voice, Sammy decided to answer his own question. "He could hypnotize him and make him open a port to Earth. He could keep that port open and make him open a port to his home world, and bring lots of his homicidal hypnotic werewolf relatives back to Portalia. Then he could take all the homicidal lunatics to Earth."

I thought about the dungeon, about how I'd stared Harold down defiantly. I'd had no idea how powerful he was. Could I resist him the next time?

"But he can't find us here, right?" I asked.

"He has hundreds of dogs out tonight, Jacob," Beverly said. "I came to warn you as soon as I could. I don't think he knows about me, not yet, but I had to be careful, just in case. I wasn't followed, I'm sure, but once they find your trail it will lead them here."

Her words only worsened the panic blooming within me. And she wasn't finished.

She wrung her hands fitfully. "There's something, someone else. You have to understand. For the longest time, he thought that Harold was the one in the legend."

"That doesn't surprise me. He's always been gullible," Bringelkoopf said.

"I know he has," Beverly said, "but the legend says 'a son will return to the place of his father's birth.' And Harold's family returned after many years of exile."

I hated to admit it, but she had a point.

The words tumbled out as she unburdened the horribly bad news. "They've found a boy at Kalatria. He opened a port, though it was a weak one. Grolfshin said it barely flickered. Harold was on his way to meet him. But when he saw the way the flute glowed at Jacob's touch, he began to think Jacob might be the one."

"The flute glowed?" I asked.

"Yeah, dude, it did," Sammy said. "It was cool, at least, I thought so then. Now, not so much."

I'd wondered at the look on Harold's face. It wasn't because of my music, it was because I'd connected with the flute and caused it to glow, just like the rock in my clubhouse.

Beverly had more. "Grolfshin said when Harold saw the way Jacob opened that port in the dungeon, a port he never knew existed, he knew that Harold would stop at nothing to get his hands on Jacob. But he is still having the boy from Kalatria brought to him. He'll have him within a few hours."

"Did Grolfshin say to where this boy's port opened?" Michael asked.

"Harold's world," Beverly whispered.

A cold darkness gripped my soul.

"Did he bring anyone through?" Michael asked.

"No, it was too weak. But with the device...." She didn't need to finish the sentence.

"Would it work?" I asked.

"No, I don't think so." Michael sounded far less certain than I would have liked.

"You don't *think* so?" Sammy asked. "So you're saying that it *might?*"

"The power of a unicorn is to sustain, not to create," Michael said. "The device should not be able to cause a weak, flickering port to open and remain open."

"But you don't know?" Sammy persisted.

"Sadly, I have not experimented with the body parts of my dead friends."

Sammy cringed and Michael rushed to apologize. "Sammy, I'm sorry." His voice was as soft as it had been harsh seconds ago. "The truth is, I have never had to contemplate something so horrific."

"Yeah, I get that," Sammy said. "I'm sorry too."

Bringelkoopf crawled up Michael's shoulders and curled around his neck. I wondered if Michael knew how much his body relaxed when his cranky companion sat on his shoulders. Or how his eyes always sparkled when the not-a-ferret was with him.

"So," Sammy asked, "why does Harold need Jacob if he has this other boy?"

"Unlike permanent ports, closed ports are extremely dangerous," Michael explained. "There is a powerful energy in the spaces between universes. Turbulent and unpredictable, like a violent storm with gusts of hurricane-force winds. It takes great strength and precision to open a stable port, one that does not slam shut unexpectedly. Even Prantos only barely had that kind of ability.

"Jacob has the ability to open a stable port to any world in the universe. It would take Harold a hundred years to find a handful of children capable of opening weak, flickering ports to a handful of worlds. With Jacob, he will not have to wait to carry out his plans."

"And what are his plans?" Sammy asked.

"In his letter, King Prantos said the Helxin family promised him they would wreak vengeance upon all humans, both on Earth and on Portalia. But King Prantos seemed to think that the Helxin family's quest for revenge would soften over five hundred years."

"Guess he was wrong," Sammy said. "But Beverly said he's getting ahold of that other boy. If Jacob's the one he needs, why even bother with the other kid?"

Mr. Korsen looked equally perplexed. "Beverly, where are they taking the boy?"

"To the Earth port."

"But I thought he didn't know where it was," I said.

"She means your father's old port, Jacob," Bringelkoopf said softly.

"Do you think he can open it?" I asked.

"I don't think so," Michael said. It hadn't been reassuring the first time he said it; it was even less reassuring now.

Sammy furrowed his eyebrows. "Once he has Jacob, he'll still need more devices. Maybe that's why Grolfshin's trying to get to other continents."

It was such a sickening thought that it took me several seconds to fully comprehend what Sammy'd said. It did not take Mr. Korsen so long.

"He'll kill every unicorn on Unicorn Isle."

"I could close my father's old port, couldn't I? I mean shut it permanently?" I asked.

"He has guards posted, Jacob. And there are so many dogs out tonight," Beverly said.

"But if that boy can open the port...." I could not bring myself to finish the question.

Michael leapt abruptly to his feet. "Jacob, you must return to Earth. He cannot get his hands on you. He could use you to take out his vengeance on all of humanity."

"He's right. You should go," Beverly said

"But what about everyone else?" I asked.

"Jacob, you need to leave in order to protect your people," Michael said. "Harold and Grolfshin could use you to do horrible, horrible things to them, and to others."

A very big part of me wanted to leap at the idea. I stared longingly toward the front door and the steps that could lead me away from evil, hypnotic, homicidal werewolf lunatics and back to the safety of my clubhouse. To the safety of Jimmy's bullying and the twins' peskiness. Back to a place where I could hide behind Sammy.

Maybe all those years of perfecting the art of hiding were going to pay off after all.

"But what about the boy? What if he can open that port?" Sammy asked.

"I will get some men and we will intercept him," Mr. Korsen said.

"And I will ask the unicorns to shut that port, permanently," Michael said.

"What about Harold's powers?" I asked

"I will take care of Harold," Michael said. "He cannot hypnotize me."

"You? I thought you could not interfere."

Michael avoided my eyes. "It is too high a price to pay, Jacob."

"So, is this how it works?" I asked. "A King protects his people by abandoning them? By leaving them at the mercy of a tyrant, and fleeing to safety?"

"Is this how I protect my people?" I asked Mr. Korsen. "By having *you* capture that boy, to keep Harold from capturing *me*?"

"Yes, Jacob, it is," he said. Like Michael, he avoided my eyes.

"Jacob," Sammy said. "They're right. You are a danger to all of them, all of us."

Two days ago, I'd not known of Portalia. Yet now, not only did I know of Portalia, but everyone was saying that I was the most dangerous thing for her.

"And you, Michael, what about you?" I asked.

But Michael had stopped being a part of the conversation. He stared down at the still-forming statue he cradled tenderly in his hands, brushed his fingers across it and smiled.

"Michael?" I asked again.

"Timing, Jacob. Timing is everything."

Sammy nodded. "The timing's just wrong, Jacob."

Michael shook his head and smiled. And at that moment the hall door flung open and the course of my life changed forever.

For Sammy was wrong. The timing had been right. Just right.

A KING IS BORN

"IT'S HERE!" MILOKAH SHOUTED. Almost instantaneously the quiet tension in the room was shattered by an angry wail as my sister's baby told the entire world of its arrival.

"What is it?" I asked.

Milokah grinned from ear to ear. "It's a boy," he said. Then he spun and left abruptly, shutting the door behind him, taking with him the sound of my nephew's cries.

"Happy birthday, Jacob." Michael's eyes had regained their usual twinkling warmth.

"Huh?"

"It's just past midnight. It's your birthday."

"He's got the same birthday as me." I grinned, all thoughts of fleeing from evil suspended until further notice.

Michael's lips curved into an all-knowing smile. He had a secret, and he hadn't finished telling it. "Yes, you were both born on the fifth day of Portal Week."

He took a moment to blow an accumulation of sawdust from his statue. Then he rubbed his huge thumb across a massive wing. "You share the same date of birth." He watched my reaction closely as he added, "As well as the same, exact time."

From the look in Michael's deeply swirling eyes, and the gaping disbelief on the faces of Beverly and Mr. Korsen, I could tell that this timing was somehow extremely important.

Michael's bemused laughter accompanied me every time I turned to stare at the hall door. Which I must have done at least a thousand times before it finally opened.

Teleana glowed with the radiant pride of new motherhood. I stared in awe.

Milokah darted out from behind her and ran into Beverly's arms.

For the first time since I'd met Milokah, my eyes did not follow him. They were riveted to the baby in my sister's arms. I was an uncle and he was my nephew.

I had a strong, burning need to hold my nephew, which surprised me. I'd never liked babies, especially after my mom brought the twins home. Babies cried and smelled funny.

But I desperately wanted to hold this one.

Teleana eased herself gingerly onto the bench beside me. "Would you like to hold him?"

When I nodded, she placed her precious bundle into my nervous, outstretched arms.

He looked sort of like a squashed prune. The most perfect squashed prune ever. I stared dumbfounded at this tiny thing, wrapped snugly in blankets with only his head poking out.

As I gazed into his bright blue eyes I knew with a certainty that it was no accident that he and I were sitting together at that moment.

The baby I held in my arms would save me. And he had a destiny which was, perhaps, even more fantastic than my own. Of that I was certain.

He made the cutest little singing noises with every breath. I grinned. I liked him.

"What's his name?"

"Morgard, Morgard Jacob."

I jerked my head up in surprise. "Jacob?"

"It is tradition for fathers to choose the first name, and mothers the second," Teleana said. "My husband decided on Morgard months ago, but not until the moment Ma told me he was a boy did I know the name I would give him. Because of you, little brother, my son was not born in a dungeon. Because of you, my son will not be taken from me. Because of you, my son has a future and a hope. I want him to have your name."

"Telly, I...." I swallowed a lump in my throat. She didn't know. She didn't know that Grolfshin had hundreds of dogs hunting for our scents. She didn't know that I was a far greater danger to her son than our uncle.

Michael set a bowl in front of Teleana. Like Sammy, I began to suspect that Michael thought food could cure anything. But it couldn't cure the threat of danger.

I stared at tiny Morgard, stroked his soft face, felt his warm skin, and listened to his little singing noises. I hadn't known babies could hum that way.

Milokah was watching me. When I looked over at him, he slipped off Beverly's lap and sat beside me.

He wrapped his arm around my waist. And when he slid his other hand around Morgard, I threaded my fingers through his and together we held our nephew.

Milokah leaned against me, and I rested my head against his. My heart thrummed wildly. We were in a room full of people, and we weren't hiding. We didn't have to. Because nobody seemed to find it odd that Milokah and I were holding hands.

"He's got your mouse ears," Milokah said. "Hopefully he'll grow into them a little faster than you did."

I knew then, what it was about Milokah. He was the stars to my soul, the dance to my song. Except, he wasn't little pinpoints of light in the distance, he was sitting right beside me. I could dance with him without ever having to move a muscle.

In his presence, the music of my soul surged. Not the music I'd been playing for years, but the music I'd always known I could play, one day, when I grew into my ears. The music of a boy who fits his soul.

Sitting beside Milokah, I was growing into my ears in leaps and bounds.

It was a moment, a perfect moment.

If it weren't for the hounds, it could have been the most perfect moment of my life.

I thought about the emotional roller coaster of the last few days.

First, I'd found out that my father had been the King. Then I'd found out that I was supposed to be the King. Then I'd found out I had an uncle, who, by the way, was doing horrible things.

I'd also learned I could manipulate the fabric of space. And that I was the fulfillment of a several-thousand-year-old legend. One that had been written by unicorns.

Now I had a sister and a nephew. And an evil man, descended from murderous lunatics and werewolves wanted to capture me, my sister, and my nephew. That same man had killed a unicorn to steal its power and was controlling my uncle, the one who currently sat on my throne.

Not to mention, I was head over heels in love.

And I had only just turned twelve.

As Milokah and I clutched Morgard closely, I thought of my uncle. How could Grolfshin have done what he did to me? I could never do such a thing to Morgard. Except that, according to Michael, Harold had a power that could make me do horrible things to my nephew.

"Morgard," I whispered, "I love you. I promise to protect you. As your King, I swear it."

I could have held him there forever, side by side with Milokah. But Ma came over.

"Jacob, hand the little one over to me, love."

She moved him into a better light and pulled back his blankets. As soon as she did, I realized that what I had thought were cute humming noises were really the sounds of Morgard struggling to breathe.

He looked like an asthmatic who'd just run a sprint and forgotten his inhaler. With every breath he took in, his belly sank in and his ribs jutted out. And with every breath he let out, he made that little singing noise. Except that it didn't sound so cute anymore.

Teleana let out a strangled sob.

"Don't worry, dear," Ma said. But her eyes were filled with tears.

Milokah buried his face in my chest. I wrapped my arms around him, not sure who was comforting who more.

"Why can't he breathe right?" I asked.

Mr. Korsen spoke with a gentleness he'd never before used with me. "The same thing happened with her first two. Their lungs just weren't ready yet. They both died within a day. It may be a mercy. It's better than being raised in a dungeon."

"Breskin," Ma said. But by the look on her face, I knew that she did not disagree.

Time slowed for me. I spun in a circle and looked at everyone.

Morgard, I'd promised to protect him, yet he might not make it through tomorrow.

Mr. Korsen, a man who had wrapped himself tightly in a cloak of anger.

Ma, the woman who had to hold everyone together.

Teleana, my sister, who had lost two children already.

Milokah, who saw something in me that I could not. Whose eyes had done things to my heart that nobody else's ever had.

Sammy, my faithful, devoted friend. He'd loved me even when I hadn't.

Beverly, who loved my uncle, and refused to give up on the man she knew he could be.

Bringelkoopf, Michael's furry version of Sammy.

And Michael. Living with humans for hundreds of years, he must have loved and lost so many. But it was not pain, sadness, or loss that I saw on my powerful, wise, several-hundred-year-old-non-human friend's face. It was fear.

And that wise, powerful, several-hundred-year-old non-human was telling me that the best thing I could do for my people was to leave them. Because the danger was too great.

"Jacob, do something, please." Milokah searched my eyes, begging me to be the person he knew me to be.

I knelt before Teleana. "Look at me. Morgard isn't going to die. I won't let him."

"Don't you dare," Mr. Korsen said. "She's been through enough."

But I had made a promise to Morgard a few moments ago.

And I was about to learn the price I would have to pay to keep that promise.

It was my twelfth birthday, and though I did not yet realize it, minutes ago I had held in my arms the very first person born during my reign as King of Portalia.

"Mr. Korsen, Morgard isn't going to die. I am going to take him to Earth."

HOME IS WHERE THE HEART IS

"BUT, JACOB, TELEANA'S not from Earth," Sammy said.

"So what?"

Sammy looked at me like it was obvious. Maybe it should have been, I realized, as he explained, one finger at a time. "She doesn't have ID. She doesn't have insurance. She doesn't have a Social Security number. As far as Earth is concerned, she doesn't exist. You can't take her to a hospital."

While Sammy listed all the hurdles standing in my way, Michael calmly plopped a dusty old shoebox on the table and rifled through it. Then, with the triumphant gleam of a magician producing a rabbit from a hat, he handed me two sets of paper.

"Your mother, she will know what to do. Just give her these."

Birth certificates and Social Security cards for Janet and William Smith.

"Your father said Smith is a common name on Earth."

"Yeah, it is," I said. "But why two?"

"Telly should not go without her brother."

Her brother. Milokah. I was stunned, it was too good to be true.

"You should go now. Before the dogs find your scent," Michael said. Something in his tone told me I wasn't going to like his next words. "Jacob, when you get to Earth, you must shut the port permanently."

"But if I close it permanently, how will I come back? I thought you said it wasn't possible to build a port from Earth."

"It isn't that it *cannot* be done, just that it has never been done. But you have such strength, Jacob. I am confident that next year, during Portal Week, you will be able to build a port from Earth to Portalia."

In my short time on Portalia, I had learned to read the wide variety of twinkles, sparkles, and swirls in the eyes of my non-human friend. Which was how I knew that Michael was lying.

"I will go with you and wait there until I see that it is closed," Michael added. "And then I will take care of Harold."

This time, I could not read his eyes.

"Then why do I need to shut my port?" I asked suspiciously. "Why can't I just close it, wait a bit, then reopen it and come back?"

"Jacob, I did not know." Michael sounded so mournfully apologetic that I knew I was missing something. "I should have sent you back at once. I did not know."

Unfortunately, Sammy didn't miss a thing. He was unable to keep the escalating fear out of his voice. "He's not sure he's strong enough to beat Harold. And Talarcos may have brought back more than just Harold and his brother. There could be dozens of them."

I waited eagerly for Michael to tell Sammy he was wrong, but he didn't.

"Then I'll take all of you. Please!"

"No," Michael said. Leaving no room for discussion, he steered us out the door.

The minute we stepped outside, my ears were assaulted by the howls of the searching hounds. My fingers flicked madly and my hands flapped twice before I was able to still them.

Mr. Korsen led me to the smallest of the waiting horses, one who, thankfully, was not quivering with fear.

"Her name is Windy." He kissed her velvety nose. "Because she runs like the wind."

Windy was not like the horse that Grolfshin's men had thrown me upon. Her eyes were sweet and gentle, and she whinnied softly when I ran my fingers along her neck.

Michael snuggled Morgard into his shirt and mounted another horse while Sammy scrambled up behind Milokah onto a third, and Teleana crawled up behind me on Windy. Michael and Mr. Korsen clasped hands, and I shuddered, for I saw fear in both their eyes.

"Come," Michael said, "let's go." He nudged his horse onwards and the others followed.

But Windy stopped at the sound of Mr. Korsen's voice. "Jacob, wait."

He leaped nimbly onto his skittish black mare, then looked me directly in the eye.

"He was my friend. I hated him for leaving us."

"I know." I held out my hand. "Until we meet again."

His handshake was not quite like Michael's had been, that first day on Portalia, but it held a grudging respect all the same. It was a beginning. Or at least, I hoped it was a beginning.

"Good luck, Jacob," Mr. Korsen said.

He slapped Windy on the rump and she took off like a rocket. I barely managed to grab her mane in time to keep from falling off.

We quickly caught up with the others, and soon we were in the lead. Mr. Korsen had been right. She ran like the wind.

We rode hard, racing to save the lives of people on two planets. For if Harold found the port that I'd carelessly left open when I came to Portalia, it would not matter that he had neither me nor the boy from Kalatria.

I should have been relieved. How hard would it be for Mr. Korsen to intercept that boy? And surely Michael could resist Harold's hypnosis? Even Bringelkoopf had been unnerved by Michael's display of fury. Unnerved, but not surprised. Surely he could resist Harold?

I glanced over at Michael. For five hundred fifty years he had walked that fine line between non-interference and interference and never faltered. Watching loved ones make mistakes that had cost them their lives.

He said every man must choose his own destiny. Non-interference, and all the pain that came with it, was the destiny he had chosen for himself. A lump rose in my throat.

Yes, Michael could stop Harold, but at what price? He would forsake his destiny and his very soul, by interfering. And though he insisted it was what he wanted to do, I could not let him.

The hoof beats of all three horses drummed as one, with a unity of purpose. The rhythm moved through me and filled my soul with the music of Portalia. And I knew what I must do.

Michael had been right about many things. Each man must choose his own destiny. But about me returning to Earth, Michael had been very, very wrong.

All my life, I'd been hiding, waiting to grow into my ears. But hiding was the very thing that had prevented me from growing into my ears.

Until a few hours ago, I'd been terrified about what would happen when Sammy discovered that I was gay. So terrified that I'd denied Milokah. So terrified that I'd denied Sammy. So terrified that I'd denied my own truth, denied my very self.

How was racing from my duty as King any different? How would I ever grow into my ears or my soul if I kept hiding?

Hiding would keep me a small mouse with big ears, a small boy in a big soul. Hiding was for mice, not men.

My destiny was not to hide in safety on Earth. My destiny was to be my people's King.

I knew next to nothing about being a King, but this much I did know—Kings do not run to hide in safety while their people battle to defend themselves.

The clearing loomed ahead, and within seconds, we arrived at the shimmering tree.

My whole body was numb from the ride. I barely managed to keep upright as Teleana and I slid off Windy's back.

Michael handed Morgard to his anxious mother, then turned to me and Sammy. "Hand me the reins. I will take the horses."

Sammy eagerly complied and dashed toward the gloriously beckoning shimmering tree. Milokah held back to see what I would do.

I gazed longingly at that shimmer. On the other side would be my mother, whose cooking I suddenly missed. And the twins and Rick, who suddenly didn't seem so horrible.

"Jacob, come on," Sammy said.

"Just a moment. I have to say goodbye," I lied. I couldn't afford to let Michael in on my plans just yet.

I patted Windy softly. "I'm sorry" I whispered, "but I still need you."

"You need to go now, Jacob," Michael said.

"What if I can't open a new port from Earth? Nobody's ever done it before. What if it isn't possible?" For surely, if it had been, wouldn't one of the humans who had been banished to Earth have tried?

"I am certain you will be able to do it," Michael said. "I'll meet you here, this time next year. I promise you."

Yes, he was definitely lying. I could see it in his eyes.

The eager howls of the fast-approaching hounds resonated through the clear night sky and even Windy began to twitch and jump.

I swallowed nervously, though not for the reason I gave Michael. "It might take me a few moments to figure out how to shut the port."

"I will not leave until it is closed, I promise. But you must go now."

"Thank you, my friend."

Casting Windy's reins to Michael, I grabbed Teleana's hand and nodded to Sammy and Milokah. "Let's go."

Sammy needed no further encouragement. I blinked and he and Milokah disappeared.

It was time. But as I lifted my foot towards the shimmer, I was overcome with fear and doubt. Once I was on the other side, would I have the courage to come back? I was a hider, and hiding was my nature.

Again I heard that voice from deep within me. "You are that person, my son. You have to be. These are your people. This is your destiny."

The voice was right. These were my people. And this was my destiny.

So, squeezing Teleana's hand tight, I led my sister and her son through to Earth.

I would have thought that by the time I found myself stepping through a shimmering tree from a planet in a parallel universe and into my clubhouse, nothing would surprise me.

I would have thought wrong.

It wasn't finding my mom and Rick waiting that surprised me. I'd had a sneaking suspicion that when we didn't show up for my birthday dinner, our absence might be noticed.

It was who was *not* there that surprised me. There were no policemen, dutifully taking a missing person's report. Sammy's mother was not there, fawning over herself with worry over her missing son. Sadly, though, her absence was not so very surprising.

But even more bewildering was the complete lack of any reaction from Mom or Rick.

I had disappeared without a trace. I expected my mom to yell at me, or grab me up in a hug and tell me how glad she was to see me alive. You know, typical "I thought you'd run away or been kidnapped" kinds of responses.

Instead, she perched on the edge of my clubhouse sofa with Rick beside her. I barely had time to note that both their eyes were red from crying.

Mom held a leather bundle in her lap. Her fingers twisted and turned one of the edges while she stared blankly at no one in particular. The bundle looked eerily similar to the one that had held the flute I'd been unable to resist.

"I wasn't sure you'd be coming back," she said. Her voice was numb. Milokah tugged at my sleeve. "Jacob, you need to shut the port."

"Yeah, I know." I suddenly realized I did not have a clue how to do what needed to be done. Morgard's noisy breathing helped me to focus.

"Mom," I said, "this is Morgard. He needs help."

I'm not sure my mom had seen any of the others until I spoke. Because when I did, she leapt up, almost dropping the leather bundle onto the floor in her haste as she rushed to Morgard.

She peered at Morgard for only a second, though, before turning and studying Teleana closely. With a strange, but not unhappy, smile, she said the most surprising thing of all. "Teleana, you look so very much like your father. You have his cheekbones, and his eyes. And his smile, definitely his smile."

My jaw literally hung open. So did Sammy's. Not only did she know who Teleana was, but it was also the first time I'd ever heard her speak about my father.

Sammy was quick to recover from the shock. He handed the bundles of papers to my mom. "Michael said you'd be able to help."

Mom nodded, and then she looked at me for the first time.

The funny thing about mothers is that they know you. And my mother knew me.

She stood with one hand atop Teleana's, and read my face.

I squirmed under her gaze, and gestured towards Milokah. "This is Milokah."

Mom didn't really seem to hear me. Instead, she retrieved the leather bundle from the sofa, and with a sad but knowing smile, held it out to me. "He always told me that it would be yours one day, but I didn't want to believe it."

She struggled to hold back her tears. "I can see it in your eyes. You are your father's son. I was wrong to try to hide it from you. I should have known that I could never keep you from your destiny. I tried to force him, I never should have, if only...."

That's when it dawned on me. My mom had blamed herself for my father's death. She must have hoped fervently that by hiding the truth from me, she could protect me.

"Mom, it wasn't your fault. He knew what he was doing. It was no accident."

"What?"

"I don't have time, now, but Sammy can explain. Dad died to protect his people, Mom, all of his people. It had nothing to do with whether or not you would move to Portalia." I peered into her eyes. "It was not your fault," I repeated.

I saw it in her face. It was like I'd lifted a heavy anchor from her drowning soul. She flung her arms around me and sobbed.

I wanted to stand there and bury my face against her chest and hold tight. But snarling hounds were descending rapidly upon the port. And I had a destiny to fulfill.

Mom bit back a strangled sob and pulled away from me.

"Mom?"

"It's okay, Sweetie. I know. You're leaving. You're going back to Portalia."

"What?" Sammy asked.

"What?" Teleana cried out.

Milokah showed no surprise, though. He smiled knowingly and tears rolled down his face.

Only a day ago, I'd said he was nobody, just some kid. But he wasn't nobody; he was the opposite of nobody. He was my soulmate. I couldn't walk away without making sure he knew that I would never again hide who he was to me, like I had in the meadow.

I wondered if it was possible to find your soulmate at twelve? As Michael had said Prios men were known to do? Milokah's eyes told me the answer was yes.

I brushed away his tears, right there in front of Mom and Rick and Sammy. Then I took his hands in mine and rested my forehead against his.

Time seemed to halt as we stood together. I wanted to savor his presence. I wanted to capture that moment, to etch the memory of our connection into my soul just in case...

Then I noticed something. As I stood with Milokah, preparing to face down Harold, my fingers, like the rest of me, were calm. They weren't searching for anything, as they always do. Because they were content simply to be in Milokah's hands.

If I could have stayed there, frozen, for eternity, I would have.

Milokah pulled his head away from mine so I could gaze in his eyes.

For so many years, I'd been waiting to grow into my ears. I'd gotten used to waiting. I'd gotten comfortable being a small mouse who hid behind Sammy.

But Milokah made me ready to fit my ears. It wasn't just that he believed in me. He saw into my very soul, in a way nobody else had, or could. And when he looked into my eyes his soul told mine that he saw a boy who was already a perfect fit for his soul, and his ears.

"You said that I would be a great King," I told him. "I thought you were wrong, that I wasn't that person. But you were right. I *am* that person. And I need to go *be* that person."

"I know."

Before I could change my mind, he kissed me softly on the cheek, and left me to sit by the piano with Telly.

That's when I saw my shiny orange-and-red tinted rock, perched atop the piano in its familiar resting spot. I darted over to collect it, as if by holding it close I could hold onto the people I loved. My heart seemed to think that was true, for once my fingers wrapped around it, there was not a power in the universe that could have pried it from them.

My eyes flicked once more to Milokah before I turned to Sammy.

"I'll take care of him," Sammy said.

I nodded and looked in the direction of the house, and the twins.

"I'll take care of them too, I promise. I kept you safe, didn't I?"

"Yes, you did, and you still do. And now I need to go and return the favor."

"Don't go!" Sammy blurted. "Please, Jacob, let them take care of it." His voice spoke the words and his heart spoke the pain, but his eyes spoke something different. His eyes told me that he knew I was not the Jacob I had been three days ago.

"I mean, it's only your destiny, right?"

"Yeah."

"You know, all those years playing that violin, you really did suck."

"Thanks."

"But you never stopped. That's your super talent, Jakey, you never give up. You never quit. And…"

"And?"

"Until I met you, nobody thought I could do anything. But you believed in me. You looked at me like there was nothing I couldn't do. You made me believe in myself, you made me want to be the person you thought I was. That's how much power you have, Jacob."

It was a good-bye speech. It was *really* a good-bye speech. For so long, I'd been worried about losing Sammy. It had been my biggest fear. And it was coming true.

I stared at the shimmering tree. The last time I had stood in that spot, I'd leapt into the unknown, safe and secure in the knowledge that my friend waited for me on the other side.

"So, I guess I'll see you next year?" Sammy said.

"Yeah, next year." I lifted my foot.

"Wait." It was Rick.

I turned, shocked, as my stepfather gathered me into his arms and hugged me tight. I had never felt his arms around me, not once, not like this.

"Jacob, I'm sorry, I never meant…it's just, you look just like him. And I was so worried about you, we were so worried. I'm sorry. Please forgive me."

And then it hit me. All that talk about me being soft, needing to grow a backbone, boarding up the clubhouse. Everything they'd said, they were worried. Because they knew I would have to face something like Harold one day. Without Sammy.

Rick pushed me back so he could look at me, and even ruffled my hair affectionately. "I'm proud of you, Jacob. Your mom and I are both very proud of you."

I nodded, terrified that if I didn't leave at that moment, I never would. Because I was starting to believe that Rick had really meant it, all those times he'd said he loved me as his own.

But I need not have worried. For I had a best friend who had always been willing to do absolutely anything for me.

Which is why, as I stared at the tree, Sammy placed his hand firmly on my back and shoved me towards the shimmer. We both knew, for me to follow my destiny, I had to walk away not only from my best friend, but also from the boy who had stolen my heart.

The last thing I heard as I stepped through the shimmer, the leather bundle clutched in one hand, the glowing orange-and-red tinted rock in the other, was Sammy.

"Happy birthday, Jacob."

DESTINIES AND PLANS

WHEN MY FOOT touched down onto the mossy ground of Portalia's forest I was greeted by an eerie silence that caused three thoughts to spring to my mind.

First, Michael was nowhere in sight. That thought was too terrifying, so my brain switched to something less threatening.

Second, it was my birthday and for the first time in twelve years, I would not be eating my birthday cake. The one my mom made every year, quite possibly the best cake ever.

Third, my missed birthday cake truly had to be the least of my concerns. I was about to try to defeat a hypnotic tyrant, one who, incidentally, seemed bent on the complete destruction of not one, but two, worlds. Yet the thought at the forefront of my brain was missing out on my well-deserved birthday cake.

I forced my brain back to the first and most pressing thought, that Michael was gone, and I immediately wished I'd allowed my brain to remain on the birthday cake.

I had a nagging feeling that there was something else missing, something else I'd expected to be there that wasn't. Two seconds later, the crisp silence was shattered by an onslaught of howling. Ah yes, that was it. The sounds of the foaming, snarling beasts hot on my trail.

Unfortunately, unlike Michael, they were not missing at all and in fact, sounded uncomfortably close. Especially considering the absence of my powerful non-human friend.

Terror gnawed at my rapidly crumbling confidence. My brain bombarded me with thousands of reasons why I should turn and leap back through the shimmering tree.

Before I could give in to the temptation, I forced my soul to focus on the port, the one and only link to my entire life as I had known it. With an agonizing roar, I slammed it shut and boarded it up.

As I stared numbly at the still, no longer shimmering tree, my legs buckled beneath me and I collapsed. For at the very moment I'd boarded up the port, I'd begun to wonder if perhaps my brilliant plan to save my people might, in actuality, be not so brilliant after all.

I was the only thing standing between all of Portalia and unspeakable horrors at the hands of the yellow-eyed, hypnotic Harold. While his hounds were closing in on me, the two friends on whom I had relied so heavily were nowhere in sight.

Clutching the leather bundle and the orange-and-red rock to my belly, I moaned until I ran out of air. And then I stopped moaning, for my lungs refused to expand.

Suddenly, I felt hands upon me. I flailed earnestly against them.

But though I could not see through the water in my eyes, I could still smell. And what I smelled was the comforting scent of cinnamon, apples and something else.

I relaxed, and as huge, gentle hands picked me up and pulled me against a familiar chest, I heard an equally familiar, yet uncharacteristically unsarcastic voice in my ear.

"Breathe," it whispered.

"Breathe," came the voice again.

Only this time, I heard not just one voice, but the combined voices of thousands whose futures depended on me. I gasped and filled my lungs with the air they so desperately needed.

Then I curled up in strong, comforting arms, and allowed myself to be carried away from the still, quiet, and very-much-not-shimmering tree. I relished the soft, furry warmth of the not-a-ferret around my shoulders, and even found comfort in the obnoxious click-clack of claws against anxious ferret teeth. I only wished I could have stayed in that moment forever.

When I heard Windy's greeting whinny, I knew the moment was over. As Michael boosted me onto Windy, I vowed to myself that I would never cry on anyone's shoulder again.

Michael swung himself onto his own horse. "You should have remained on Earth."

"You mean where I would be safe while you protected my people?"

"Yes."

"You said that non-interference was your duty, your destiny."

"Each man chooses his own destiny, his own path, Jacob. I chose mine."

"And I've chosen mine. These are my people. I will not scurry to safety and leave them at the mercy of a tyrant."

"Hate to break up the reunion," Bringelkoopf interrupted, "but is it just me, or do the snarling, vicious, drooling, and probably rabid hounds sound like they are getting closer?"

I gripped Michael's elbow. "Do not forsake your conscience for me. I beg you, as a friend. Stay true to your own destiny, and allow me to do the same. You told me that my strength was that I listened to my soul. That is what I do now."

"Have you ever smelled snarling hound breath?" Bringelkoopf asked. "I tell you, just before they clamp their jaws around you, it is the most foul, awful smell. But hey, don't take my word for it, sit around and chat a bit longer. You'll see for yourselves."

Michael chuckled, and his eyes sparkled with rainbow-colored glitter. It was only then that I realized that he had his horse, I had mine, but the others were gone.

"You knew I'd come back?"

He did not answer, but gestured to the bundle my mother had given me. "What's that?"

I handed it to him. "She said it was my father's and that now it is mine."

He peeled back the leather as though it were fine wrapping paper, revealing a deep purple cloth with an orange-and-red emblem embroidered on the front.

His breath caught in his throat. "The King's cloak has been worn by every King since the time of the Great Shutting. It was gifted to King Prantos the First by the Great Unicorn Fredriko. Your mother was right. It was your father's and now it is now yours."

Bringelkoopf cleared his throat. "Getting closer, just in case you hadn't noticed."

Michael stroked the embroidery on the cloth. "Yes, Jacob, I knew you would come back. You are your father's son. I had no doubt."

He tried to return the bundle to me, but I shook my head.

"Not while my people are still in danger," I told him.

Before he could respond, I clucked to Windy and started off, buying myself a few moments alone with my thoughts as we raced into the night. My father's cloak reminded me of Grolfshin's. Except Grolfshin's had no orange-and-red emblem on it.

As we rode, I had a waking dream about the cowering purple puppy and the snarling wolf with red fur and yellow eyes. Only this dream was different. The purple puppy had an orange-and-red emblem on his chest. The emblem began to glow as if on fire and the purple puppy stood up tall and smiled. For he had grown into his ears, and he was no longer cowering.

* * *

When the howls of the hounds seemed distant enough, we stopped.

"I have a plan," I said.

Michael raised a skeptical eyebrow.

"Really?" Bringelkoopf asked. "And what is your... plan?"

"I'm gonna let Harold capture me."

"Ah, brilliant. What a relief. I must say, those dungeon floors are most comfortable. For a moment, I was worried your plan involved something that would force us to spend a night in one of those uncomfortably luxurious castle beds. Phew."

I scratched his chin, but deftly withdrew my fingers before his cute, adorable not-a-ferret teeth had a chance to playfully nip.

Michael frowned. "Jacob, you do not know if you can resist his eyes."

I lifted the orange-and-red rock to my nose, and savored its familiar scent. I would think of Milokah, Freedom, and my people, and I would derive strength from their hope.

Michael's lips twitched when he saw the rock.

"In the dungeon, I caught him off guard," I said.

"You will not do so again."

"I know. I'm counting on it."

And I outlined my plan to save my people.

"Do I have your support?" I asked them.

"Yes," Michael said.

I craned my neck to Bringelkoopf.

"Do I have a choice?" he asked.

"Yes, you do."

He answered with his rare, respectful and not sarcastic voice. "Yes, my friend. Always."

"Good. So where do I send Harold?"

"Ooooh, I know. How about under the sea somewhere?" suggested Bringelkoopf.

"Raolkint," Michael said. "There are a few humans there. He would live."

"Okay. Raolkint it is."

"And Grolfie?" Bringelkoopf asked. "Will you send him to Raolkint or toss him in the dungeon?"

"Neither. One more thing, Michael." I steeled myself, but it had to be this way. "I do not want you there."

Neither of us needed me to add that I feared he would not be able to resist the temptation to interfere if things went wrong. Although he respected my decision, he could not keep the hurt, or the fear, from his face. "Alright, Jacob, if that's what you want."

"It is. I will see you tomorrow. At the castle."

"Jacob, I want you to know—"

"Tell me tomorrow."

He nodded reluctantly. "Okay, tomorrow. At the castle."

With that, he left. I watched after him and tried to calm the churning fear. "Tell me I can do this," I whispered.

"You can. I know you can," Bringelkoopf said. "I have faith in you, my friend."

As my faithful and exhausted mount carried me closer and closer toward my magnificent plan, I thought wryly that one way or the other, it would all be over soon. Suddenly, Windy screeched to a halt with a terrified squeal. She reared up on her hind legs and dumped me unceremoniously to the ground.

I called after her. But she was gone, galloping madly away as I was dragged onto my feet by two sets of very not-gentle hands.

My skin was the first to notice his presence. It started crawling as though it thought that it could leave me to save itself. My ears heard his malicious chuckle and balked with displeasure at the grating noise. I tried to protect my ears from the assault, but the very not-gentle hands would not let me move my arms.

Only after my skin had felt him and my ears had heard him did my eyes see the yellow orbs moving toward me in the darkness.

"How nice of you to join us," Harold crooned. "I was quite sure you would have scurried into hiding."

Bringelkoopf had slithered away at the first sign of Harold. But it wasn't the disappearance of my furry friend that upset me. It was the way my entire plan had taken flight the moment I'd looked into those yellow eyes.

What was my plan? Oh, yes, that's right, said a sarcastic voice inside me. Not Bringelkoopf's sarcastic voice, but Jacob's sarcastic voice. The Jacob who had always taken refuge behind his great friend and protector, Sammy, the Sammy who was on Earth.

The plan, yes, was to pretend to be terrified of Harold, so that Harold believed he had won control over me. Yes, a fantastic plan, except—my sarcastic self felt compelled to point out—there was no need to pretend to be terrified. Yep, no acting needed, none, whatsoever.

A rock plummeted to the bottom of my stomach as I realized that I had just given Harold the one thing he needed to carry out his vengeance against humanity. Me.

Harold's chuckle grew into a smug, satisfied roar. "Grolfshin, your nephew seems surprised. Why, I do believe he thought he could outwit me."

Grolfshin stepped into view beside him. "Doesn't surprise me. He's so very much like his father." But, like in the dungeon, my uncle's eyes held a strange mixture of anger, sadness, and remorse. Only this time, they also held something else—the pain of lost hope.

I wanted to tell him to hold on to his hope, that I had a plan, but I couldn't. Instead, I allowed my soul to drink its fill of the power gifted to me by the eagle Freedom. My fingers clung to my father's orange-and-red rock. I thought of Milokah. And Harold's pull on me weakened.

Remember the plan, a voice inside said. Resist those eyes, but don't let him see it.

"Come," Harold said. "You will open a door for me."

"Nnnnnnnnooooo," I muttered with as much fear and trembling as I could muster.

Harold patted my cheek. "Oh, Jacob, we both know you will."

He looked over my shoulder and said, "Bring him."

The two pairs of very not-gentle hands that were holding me hauled me off to a clearing.

I wasn't prepared for what I saw.

Mr. Korsen, Ma, Beverly, Roland Harkins, and a strange boy were all tied up next to a tree. They were guarded by four huge, ogre-like men who looked like they belonged in the dungeons. Not as prisoners, but as dungeon masters.

Roland was quivering in fear and his eyes were wide with fright. But the eyes of the boy beside him were vacant.

Ma stifled a horrified gasp when she saw me. Her eyes searched frantically behind me. This was not lost on Harold.

"Ah, yes, where are your friends, Jacob?" Harold asked.

My eyes were tethered by the magnetism of those yellow eyes. Try as I might, I could not pull them away.

Harold laughed at my efforts. His laugh conjured up visions of a small boy torturing animals while his mother knit socks and gazed adoringly at him from a porch swing.

"M...M...Michael took them, I don't know where," I stammered.

"Well, no matter. I don't need them now, do I?"

My heart surged. Harold might control my eyes, but my tongue belonged to me.

Out of the corner of my eye, I saw something furry sneak up behind Mr. Korsen and begin gnawing on the rope that bound his hands. Yes, the voice inside me said, you can do this.

Harold gestured to the tree and tossed an arm around Grolfshin's shoulders. "Grolfshin, my friend, I have waited seventeen long years for this moment."

"Seventeen?" Grolfshin's confusion was obvious.

Harold licked his lips like a cat who has cornered a mouse after a very long and enjoyable session of play, and is finally moving in for the kill.

"I had meant to do this with your grandfather. Unfortunately, Talarcos had a change of heart." He hung his head in mock sadness. "It pained me to kill him."

"What?" Grolfshin cried out.

Harold continued as if Grolfshin had not spoken. "And your brother, well, we couldn't let him spread rumors now, could we? You have only yourself to blame. Had you been able to control Prantos, I would not have had to send my brother to Earth to get rid of him. Poor Felix, he loved me so. And it cost him his life. But now that I have Jacob, I forgive you."

Harold clasped Grolfshin in a friendly embrace. "Let us call it even and put this behind us, alright my friend?"

"Yes, of course."

That settled, Harold turned back to the tree before he could see what I saw—a fire in Grolfshin's eyes which told me it was most definitely not all right.

"So, Prios," Harold said, rubbing his greedy hands together, "let's do this."

He snapped his fingers and one of the beefy ogre-men picked Roland and the other boy up by their necks and dumped them in front of Harold. Harold patted their heads, and laughed as Roland made a feeble attempt to pull away.

The other boy appeared almost comatose.

"This is my new pet from Kalatria," Harold said. "He is not as talented as you are, but I believe with enough encouragement he will be able to open the port to Earth for me. Sadly, he has not yet succeeded in getting more than a brief flicker. Still, the night is young."

At his words, the dungeon master grinned, exposing dazzling, glistening bright white teeth, which I thought seemed out of place for a dungeon master. No doubt he brushed and flossed daily. My dentist, Dr. Wergeston, would have been very, very pleased with his teeth. In fact, he probably would have let him have an extra ten minutes on the video game of his choice.

"I'll do you a deal, Jacob," Harold said, "you open this port to Earth for me, and you will not have to watch while I encourage this young man to hone his talents for me."

On cue, the dungeon master grinned and unfurled his long whip with a flick of his wrist and a mighty, ear-splitting crack.

The boy from Kalatria did not even flinch.

What had Harold done to make him so numb?

Even if that poor boy wanted to open a port, how could he? He had gone to a place far, far beyond fear. How could his soul even breathe, let alone sing?

"If you have this boy, why bother with me?"

"I desire a door to Earth. He cannot give it to me. At least, not yet." Harold shook his head. "Jacob, Jacob, you will open this port for me. The only question is whether I need to force you. But I *will* get what I want."

I hesitated for only a second and he said, "Beat the messenger boy."

Roland glanced at me, his eyes frantic with fear, and retched.

"No, I'll do it!" I cried out. "I'll do it."

"Good boy." Harold chuckled and waved off the unhappy dungeon master.

Harold thought he had scared me into doing his bidding by threatening Roland and the boy from Kalatria. But I wasn't trembling from fear, I was trembling from the awesome power that surged through my soul.

I thought of my people and my soul sang a song of Earth. The tree shimmered instantaneously.

Harold watched me with a greedy gleam in his eyes and rolled the unicorn device between his fingers in eager anticipation.

The rope sparkled in a way that made it appear to be moving on its own, as if alive and I shuddered, knowing the sparkles were caused by rays of moonlight reflecting off pieces of the dead unicorn Petros.

"Grolfshin, my friend," Harold said, "check it out for me. I need to know that it is safe. After all, you saw how decreasingly stable my pet's gates became as he grew more tired."

When Grolfshin did not jump at his command, Harold continued in a more ominous tone. "Go now, or do you, too, need more encouragement?"

"No, of course not." Grolfshin cast a quick, questioning glance in my direction, then stepped obediently through the shimmer. He was gone for only a few seconds.

When he returned, his shoulders were slumped and his smile forced. "Earth, just as I remember it."

I didn't have time to worry about my uncle. Out of the corner of my eye, I saw Harold unravel his unicorn rope, the one that would allow him to keep the port to Earth open, giving him access to weapons and technology—and to Milokah, Sammy, and Morgard.

I was about to find out whether my plan would save my people, or doom them forever.

CONQUERING THE ENEMY

HAROLD RADIATED WITH sadistic glee. Swinging his rope in bigger and bigger circles, he edged closer to the shimmering port. From the look on his face, I suspect he was already daydreaming about all the fun-filled acts of cruelty he could commit now that he had the long-sought-after doorway to Earth I'd just given him.

As Michael had said, timing is everything.

The first time he'd said it had been right after Morgard was born. The second was when we were fine-tuning my plan and he'd insisted that I should open a port to Earth first.

Michael had been right. And so far, everything was going according to plan.

Holding every fiber of my body completely still, most especially my twitchy fingers, I silently willed the port to shut.

The shimmer collapsed with a sizzling crackle, sending forth a gust of static electricity that knocked me off my feet, and caused Harold to stumble into Grolfshin.

For an entire nanosecond, Harold seemed unable to comprehend that something had happened without his permission, and very much against his will.

But Harold had not gotten this close to his goal by using only his hypnotic eyes. It did not take him long to figure out who had thwarted his plans.

He turned on me, his lips drawn back in a rictus, exposing his wolf-like teeth. Any doubts I might have had that he was descended from the werewolves of Giza vanished.

"Open it," he snarled. "Open it again now."

I cowered beneath him, and the vision of the purple puppy sprang vividly to my mind. "I'm sorry. It was an accident. You were scaring me. I couldn't help it."

He wrapped his fingers around my windpipe and dragged my forehead against his, forcing me to stare into his deranged eyes and inhale his rotten-egg-smelling breath. Splattering my face with vile foamy spittle, he pointed at Roland and roared, "Beat him until he is dead!"

The dungeon master laughed with delight and flung his arm behind him, allowing the whip to unfurl to its greatest length. The whip was very, very long. And the tip looked very, very sharp. My brain focused, once again, on the absolutely irrelevant fact that the dungeon master's teeth glistened bright white.

Mr. Korsen leapt up in a feeble attempt to stop the dungeon master. But his hands were not yet unbound, and one of Harold's other goons quickly flattened him.

"No!" I shouted desperately. "No. Please." My plan was falling apart. This was not how it was supposed to go. "I can open it again, I can. Please. I promise. Give me another chance."

"Too late." Harold's yellow eyes bore into me, and their pull was stronger than ever. I screamed in horror, both at what he intended for Roland, and at the way my feet were suddenly cemented to the ground.

I was paralyzed, unable to do anything but watch.

The dungeon master swirled his whip overhead in a wide, graceful arc and cracked it with a snap of his wrist, giving us a sneak preview of its awesome capabilities.

After warming up his arm, he narrowed his eyes on his target, Roland's back, and contorted his lips into a malicious grin.

I've heard people say that when they are faced with something hideous, such as imminent death, everything suddenly starts to move in slow motion. What I've never heard people say is that while most things slow down or even stop, like my feet did, some things, like the dungeon master's arm and whip, move faster and faster until they are almost a blur.

And that while some things slow down and some things speed up, sound stays the same. Like the sound of Roland's uncontrolled sobbing as he waited for the dungeon master's whip to sink into his back while his King stood and watched.

For I was Roland's King, and standing and watching was all I seemed to be capable of doing. I tried desperately to move. But I could not so much as wiggle my toe.

I am his King! My heart cried out as Roland's sobs deteriorated into a keening wail.

I am his King. I cannot stand and do nothing. But Harold's eyes held me paralyzed.

In futile desperation, I screamed so loud that I drowned out the sound of Harold's lunatic laughter and Roland's terrified howls. But still my legs would not even tremble, quake, or shiver.

I should have listened to Michael and Mr. Korsen. Why had I told Michael not to come with me? Now Roland was going to die because of my stupidity.

The dungeon master brought his arm forward, driving the tip of the whip like an arrow on the last leg of its journey.

Suddenly, a hard and painful realization struck me. It was no longer Harold's eyes which kept me immobilized.

It had started that way. But at some point in the last fraction of a second, his eyes had lost their hold on me. Since then my eyes had been glued to Roland's back, not Harold.

Just like when I'd let myself be consumed with fears about Sammy finding out I was gay, I was paralyzed by my own fear and nothing else.

Harold knew it and his body shook with satisfied rage.

A sudden hope surged through me. I was Roland's King and Roland's King had a choice. No, I told myself, not a choice, a duty. My duty was to protect him. At any cost.

Fiery jolts surged from the rock I clutched in my hand. In my mind I beheld a vision of an enormous orange-and-red fire-breathing dragon. I didn't understand it, but it didn't matter. Every kid knows that a dragon is a fearsome beast with thick scales, impervious to something so paltry as a dungeon master's whip.

I remembered back to Michael's cabin, when I'd realized my father had left me a legacy. I'd known with a certainty that I'd need the rock for something. Now I knew what that "something" was: to remind me I could be the person Milokah knew me to be.

Tightly gripping the rock, I ripped myself from the imaginary cement out of which my feet had refused to move.

I threw myself across Roland's back and wrapped my arms around him. I immersed myself in the memory of Milokah's smile and awaited the certain excruciating pain of the whip.

This is what Kings do, I told myself. Kings do not stand and watch. Kings protect. This is a King's destiny, and my soul knew it.

The whip snaked past my ear with a high-pitched whine.

My ears cringed and I tensed.

The whip thudded into the ground beside us with a heavy wallop.

My body bounced and huge chunks of rock flew up and smashed into my face.

I clung to Roland and waited for the pain to hit.

But the pain did not hit.

After a split second of silence, a new sound assailed my ears. The sound of an irate dungeon master. For when I'd thrown myself on top of Roland, I'd nudged us both. Not far. But far enough that the dungeon master had missed his mark. And he was not pleased.

I opened my eyes and gagged. The whip had carved out a four-inch-deep gaping rut in the rock-solid soil that would have torn halfway through my soft-as-butter back.

As the dungeon master pulled back his arm, I spun to the tree. My only hope was to get the port open before he could strike. He would surely not miss again.

My soul, knowing what was at stake, complied, and the tree shimmered brightly.

"There's the port to Earth," I told him.

But I was lying through my-not-so-pearly-white teeth. Once a portal is opened, there is only one destination at the other end. However, *before* it is opened, a portal site is merely an access point—a point with *multiple* connection possibilities.

I'd opened the portal to Earth the first time. This time, I opened it to a desolate planet called Raolkint where, according to Michael, Harold would find just enough food and water to live out a long, lonely, miserable life. Even that was more than he deserved.

But first, he had to go through the portal.

"Please! It won't happen again. I promise."

Harold considered it, then shrugged and halted the dungeon master. "See that it doesn't. Next time, I will not be so understanding."

Relief flooded me. I slumped beside Roland and watched with bated breath as Harold swirled his unicorn rope and flung it into the shimmer. It settled with a comfortable ease.

Harold beckoned to two of his goons to join him. Then, just before he stepped through, he turned to Grolfshin and said, "If he tries anything else, kill the boy."

The moment Harold and his goons disappeared through the port, I pounced on the tail end of the unicorn rope, braced myself for the searing agony I knew I would need to endure, and heaved.

I had been wrong about the searing agony. I'm not sure the dictionary has a word to describe the oh-so-not-just-agony that ripped through my body. But I didn't care. I clung to that rope and pulled with everything I had.

Grolfshin grabbed my shoulders. "What are you doing?"

"Stay back. You'll get hurt."

I glanced at the two remaining ogre-like men. My plan had not considered the possibility of any dungeon masters, let alone the two Harold had left behind.

Harold's burly oafs weren't the brightest men, but even they figured out that my pulling on the rope was probably not a part of their master's brilliant plan.

Ogre number one started toward me. "Hey, get away from there."

But Bringelkoopf had finally gnawed his way through Mr. Korsen's rope and Mr. Korsen effortlessly tackled him before he could reach me.

Unfortunately, that still left ogre number two. I had a sneaking suspicion that in a tug-of-war with him, I would lose.

"Uncie," I called out, praying that I had not misread the strange emotions I'd seen on my uncle's face. "Don't let him stop me."

Without waiting to see how he responded, I turned my attention back to the shimmer. I did not see Grolfshin, Roland, Ma, and Beverly take down ogre number two.

All I knew was that I heaved and pulled and tugged at the rope. But it would not yield.

In fact, not only did it not budge, it began to meld itself to the fabric of the portal.

Michael had not known how it worked. We'd had to make a lot of guesses. One of the guesses was that if I could not get the rope out quickly, it would never come out and I would be unable to close the port. Ever.

Closing my eyes, I blocked out the pain of burning flesh that radiated up my arm, and focused only on prying the rope from the port.

If I failed, Harold would return. He would kill Roland. He would torture the boy from Kalatria. And probably all of Portalia's children. He would find a way to Unicorn Isle so he could make more devices. And he would go to Earth.

It was now or never, and never was getting closer. I had the strength of Freedom, my father, Milokah, and the orange-and-red rock. What was I missing?

The Legend of the Unicorns sprang into my mind. I realized that the legend was not about humans. The unicorns had written a legend about Portalia's King. *Their* King.

The unicorn Petros was one of my people, just as Roland, Morgard, Milokah, and all the others were. For my destiny was to be the King of *all* of Portalia's people, not just the humans.

The Legend of the Unicorns was a song. A promise of love and freedom. Written to Portalia telling her of her people's King.

The pain that radiated through my body as I clutched the rope was the pain the unicorn Petros had felt, knowing that his body would be used against his beloved Portalia.

My father had said he needed to tune his heart with the right key for it to resonate with his soul. At first I'd thought that love was what resonated with my soul, for thoughts of Milokah had allowed me the greatest connection with my soul I'd ever had.

But it was more than love. It was being true to myself that allowed me to sing with my soul. Milokah was my truth. But my destiny was also my truth.

All my life, I'd denied my own truth. And every time I did, my soul had wilted, and I'd grown just a little bit smaller for my ears, and a little bit farther away from one day fitting my soul. And my heart had become more and more out of tune with my soul.

I knew then what it was that was preventing me from removing the rope.

I was still denying my truth.

I thought of Portalians as my people. Yet I hadn't thought of myself as Portalian. I was still thinking of myself as a kid from Earth.

But I could not be a boy from Earth. I had to be a son of Portalia, returned.

Like I'd held hands with Milokah in the clubhouse, I had to let Portalia know I would not deny her. I would not turn my back on my destiny, or my people.

In my mind, I saw a small mouse. It smiled at me, then turned tail and scurried off and disappeared. In its place, I saw only a boy who fit his ears. And Milokah's smile.

Remembering the final words of the Legend of the Unicorns, words I had heard countless times but never understood, I swore an oath to Portalia. "I will be your guardian, your portal master and your people's King. I swear it."

As soon as the words left my heart and my lips, the power of Portalia radiated through me as she shared her power with her people's King.

With a final heave on the rope, I commanded the port to shut.

The ground trembled.

A bolt of lightning surged from within and struck the ground beside me.

A thunderous, deafening boom rent the night air. The rope peeled away, spewing forth hot, molten sparks in all directions as it severed its connection with the portal.

The shimmer collapsed with an angry keening wail, sending forth a shock wave that threw me fifty feet backwards into the solid embrace of a very thick and very thorny tree.

A vague, detached part of me heard the surprised shrieks of the others as they, too bounced off an assortment of trees.

A cloud of smoke billowed from the now-closed gate, and singed rope remnants shot upwards, sputtering sparks before falling lifelessly to the ground.

The boy from Kalatria remained in his blank, detached daze, but the rest of us stared in shock. For where the tree had been was now a crater the size of a fire truck. There was absolutely no sign of Harold nor his two goons.

For several minutes, none of us dared to move.

Amazingly, Roland came around first. "Cool! What was that?"

From the tone of his voice, you would never guess that less than five minutes earlier he had narrowly escaped being flogged to death.

"Freedom," I heard myself say from somewhere that sounded so very far away.

And then I blacked out.

HER PEOPLE'S KING

TRY AS I MIGHT, I can remember only a few snapshots from the rest of that night. How we got from Harold's Crater to the castle is not one of them.

However, as Roland enthusiastically recounts the tale, I hear it involved me being toted like a sack of potatoes across Mr. Korsen's shoulders.

I vaguely remember staring at a bunch of surprised and unhappy people when I insisted that Grolfshin not be placed in the dungeon with Harold's two remaining men. Mr. Korsen was so beside himself with fury that he was, quite thankfully, speechless.

After telling my equally dumbstruck uncle that we'd talk in the morning, I dragged myself up the stairs and somehow managed to find the bed I'd slept in the night before. The last thing I remember was the sight of the pillow rushing up to meet me.

I did not dream that night. I slept. I slept until a faint, hesitant voice crept into my head.

"Your Majesty?" It was a familiar voice. But not one of my accustomed, familiar voices.

"Hey, my little cherub, he's telling you it's time to get up." Now that voice I knew.

"Sorry to wake you, Your Majesty." Manservant peered anxiously down at me. "But, ah, it's getting late, and people are waiting."

My mouth felt like it had been stuffed with cotton balls. I'd no sooner had that thought than a glass of water appeared in front of me, as if by magic, but really by Manservant.

I gulped it down greedily. "Thanks, Manservant... I mean, what is your name?"

"Nikolai, Your Majesty."

"Good morning, Nikolai. What people are waiting?"

"Your uncle desires very much to speak with you, Your Majesty."

"Really? You don't say?" crooned my favorite obnoxious pest. Though I could hardly be mad at him, as the very same words would have come from my mouth if it had not been full of water. But I wasn't going to say that to Bringelkoopf.

"Nikolai, can you hold off on the Your Majesty thing for just a little bit?"

Nikolai smiled and bowed his head. "Of course, Your Majesty. Mr. Michael waits for you. And people are gathering in front of the castle to welcome you."

"In front of the castle?"

"Yes, Your Majesty, many, many people. Might I be so bold as to make a suggestion?"

"Oh, I so wish you would, Nikolai." The words did not come out the way I'd intended and he tensed as though I'd snapped.

"No, seriously, Nikolai, I mean it, I would love a suggestion. I really would." This time my voice must have matched my intentions because he relaxed immediately.

"Well, Your Majesty, I would suggest breakfast with your uncle, then tea with Mr. Michael. The people outside will be gathering all the day long. I do not believe they expect their King to rush out to meet them."

"I'm curious, Nikolai. Why do you suggest I speak with my uncle first?"

"Is that not what weighs most heavily on your mind, Your Majesty?"

"Yes, Nikolai, it is."

Nikolai winked, and though his eyes lacked the sparkles and swirls of Michael's, I liked his wink all the same. I especially liked what he said next.

"The tub is drawn and I've laid out clean clothes. Shall I tell your uncle, say, half an hour, Your Majesty?"

"Yes, thank you, Nikolai," I said, motivated for the first time to actually get out of bed.

"You're welcome, Your Majesty." Nikolai shut the door quietly behind him.

I had a sneaking suspicion that getting him to stop calling me "Your Majesty" was a battle I would not win.

I'd never been a soak-in-the-tub kind of guy. But as I slipped into the perfectly warm, not-too-hot, not-too-cold water, I decided I could definitely get used to it. Just before I closed my eyes to savor the bliss, I noticed a small bell perched precisely within my reach.

I resisted the urge to summon Nikolai and suggest he inform everyone that His Majesty would be soaking in the tub for at least another century or two.

* * *

Breakfast smelled and looked amazing, but there was no way around the fact that the room was filled with an uncomfortable tension.

Milokah had been so right. It was easier to hate than to love. Oh, how much easier it would all have been to do what Mr. Korsen, Bringelkoopf, and indeed, most of Portalia wanted me to do—throw Grolfshin in a dungeon and throw away the key.

I thought of how desperately I'd wanted him to be the uncle I'd never had. And how angry I'd been at him for not being able to be who I wanted him to be.

Less than twelve hours earlier, I'd faced down a deranged madman and conquered my deepest fear. Compared to forgiving my uncle, that had been a breeze.

Grolfshin and I played with our food and glanced surreptitiously at each other. Neither of us ate. Every time I glanced at Grolfshin I saw that, though his eyes overflowed with pain and tears, he was building a wall around himself with every passing moment.

Soon, I was certain, I would not be able to get through, even if I wanted to.

Yet I was frozen, much as I had been at Harold's Crater. I began to think that perhaps my dream of an uncle who loved me was simply a dream I could not keep.

A loud, exaggerated throat clearing startled me out of my paralysis.

Timing, as Michael says, is everything.

"Did you have a nice bath, Your Majesty?" Nikolai replaced my cold frinkle with a fresh, warm one.

"Yes, Nikolai, I did. Thank you." I would have been thankful had he asked me about an ingrown toenail at that point, just to break the uncomfortable silence.

"So, Uncle, did you sleep well?"
"Yes, I did. And you?"
"Yes, fine, thank you."
"Oh brother, we'll be here until my whiskers fall off," Bringelkoopf grumbled.

And then I thought of Roland. He'd snapped back from the trauma of his almost-flogging as quickly as he'd leaped and bounded from the tree to the river and to the tree again. Perhaps leaping was the best way forward.

"You didn't know he'd killed your father, did you?" I asked.
"No."
"And what about mine? Did you really think he'd abandoned you?"
"I wanted to think that. More than anything. I had to believe he'd abandoned us, because if he hadn't, it would mean he was dead. And I did not want my Prantie to be dead. You have to understand, you have to believe me."

I did. I understood more than he could know.

For years I'd told myself that my dad had been abducted by aliens, or kidnapped as part of a secret government project, or even simply gotten lost.

Because if he'd left, there was always a chance that one day he'd walk through the front door again. But dead—that meant gone, never coming back. And that hurt a lot worse.

We were all we had left of my father, my uncle and I. And so I leapt.

I ran to him and he wrapped his arms around me and held me tight.

We clung to each other and cried. And finally accepted, for the very first time, that my father, his brother, was gone. He would never be coming back. Never be walking through the front door. Not ever again.

For a long time Grolfshin held me close like he had the day I'd met him. Only this time, when he whispered, "I love you, Jacob, I really do," I knew he meant it.

And when I said, "I love you too, Uncie," I knew that I meant it too.

* * *

Michael was on his third pot of tea when I met up with him.

"Sorry, I meant to be here earlier. I had breakfast with Grolfshin, and we talked."

Michael raised his eyebrow. "And?"

"It's gonna take time but I think we'll be okay."

"I think so too."

"But I don't trust him, not yet."

"No, that will take time."

"Yeah."

"So, I heard you had quite a night."

"You could say that."

"Indeed." Michael chuckled. "Young Roland was up at the crack of dawn spreading the tale through the village. To hear him tell it, you're about fifty feet tall by now, and you'll probably be more powerful than twenty dragons by the time the day is through."

I smiled. "Maybe even thirty."

The leather bundle my mother had given me rested on the table beside Michael. I knew it held my father's cloak. But my eyes were drawn to a second bundle, the one Michael was holding in his lap.

Michael's eyes showed off their full range of mischievous twinkling, with colors I'd not yet seen. He handed the second bundle to me. "Happy birthday, Jacob."

My fingers trembled. I peeled back the leather to unveil the finished statue that Michael had been skillfully carving as he told me of my history and my destiny.

I'd been wrong. Those magnificent wings were not the wings of an angel.

They were part of a statue of the majestic eagle Freedom. And me.

Freedom stood behind me, proud and fearsome, his wings outstretched to their fullest. His eyes blazed with a frightful defiance that threatened anyone who might dare to try to harm the boy he clutched against his heart.

I wore a cloak with an intricate emblem on the front. My feet rested on Freedom's talons, my head was bowed, and my hands were clasped in front of me. Together, Freedom and I stood on a rock, with a hollow concavity below our feet.

The crossed blades that Freedom gripped in his talons extended upwards along the length of my arms. "Passion" was inscribed on one blade and "Love" on the other.

"He would not have shared his strength with you if he did not think you worthy," Michael said.

At that moment I remembered the way Michael's lips had twitched when he'd seen me holding my orange-and-red rock. A tingle ran down my spine. I pulled the rock from my pocket, and placed it in the concavity at Freedom's feet.

It clicked into place, and an orange-and-red hue emanated from the wooden statue.

I peered closely at the emblem on the cloak my statue self was wearing.

"Perhaps it is time you looked at the real thing," Michael said.

A sad smile creased his face as he handed me my father's bundle. He appeared to be reliving a lifetime of memories of other men to whom he'd given this very same cloak.

I rested my hands upon the leather, closed my eyes, and took in a long, deep breath. Visions of my father, and generations of Prios men, soared through me, connecting with me, speaking to me.

And they told me it was time.

My heart raced as my fingers unwrapped my father's cloak. My eyes rested on the glorious purple fabric and its intricately embroidered emblem—a unicorn, a dragon, and a man, all three embraced within the wings of an eagle.

Michael took the cloak from me. He unfurled it, then folded it in half and arranged the heavy fabric on my shoulders. He smoothed out invisible creases and brushed off non-existent lint. When he was finished, he stepped back to admire me, like a proud father might.

"I love you, Jacob, I have always loved you," he said. "I was there the day you were born. I loved your father, and his father before him, yes. But you, you have always been so very special to me. For you, I would do anything. You are like a son to me. I want you to know that."

He tweaked my hair and, strangely, managed to find a way to get it to stay behind my ears. Perhaps his several hundred years of experience with my family had paid off.

"I placed this very same cloak on your father's shoulders. Though for him I did not need to fold it in half. He, also, thought it was too heavy a burden for him to bear. He was wrong. As are you. You have an enormous capacity for love, my friend, like none I've ever known. And your passion, I've not felt the likes of it, not ever. It knocked the wind from my lungs, the day you were born."

I leaned forward and rested my forehead on his chest, only for a moment.

Then I looked down at my father's cloak. My cloak. And my fingers traced the emblem on my chest.

I caressed the wings of the eagle.

Michael whispered, "An eagle behind him."

I moved to the regal unicorn.

"A unicorn to guide him."

Trembling with the certainty that Michael's words were not simply an inspirational burst of poetry conjured up that very moment, my fingers traveled across to the mighty dragon.

"A dragon to defend him."

That left only the figure of the cloaked man.

"A heart to sing the song of souls. On freedom's wings his spirit will soar."

The song of souls. That's what Bringelkoopf had said I needed to sing to open a port.

After a moment of silence, Michael spoke again. "It's time, Jacob."

I nodded and settled Bringelkoopf upon my shoulders.

"It's about time," he said. "I've not napped in over an hour."

Somehow, my cloak hadn't felt complete without the not-a-ferret.

Michael was right. It was time.

As I ambled slowly toward the front door, I thought about the final verse of the Legend. "For he is her guardian, the portal master, and most of all, her people's King."

One day I would be Portalia's guardian. One day, I would truly be her portal master. But first I needed to be her people's King.

With that thought, I stepped through the front door of the castle and embarked upon my journey as my people's King.

The path along which Sammy and I had walked when we'd first come to the castle, only two days ago, overflowed with people for as far as I could see. Nikolai had not been exaggerating when he told me there were many, many people.

Michael squeezed my arm encouragingly as I descended the steps. I heard hushed and excited whispers as I began my walk toward the lane.

Suddenly, it all stopped.

There was a dead silence, followed by a collective gasp of awe. People on either side of the path parted to make way. The wind was sucked from my lungs by what I saw. A unicorn was prancing down the lane toward me.

He glowed magnificently white, and the sun glared blindingly off his glass-like hooves with every step he took.

His horn was truly regal, and so much longer than I would have thought. It matched the length of his legs, yet he moved as though it were weightless upon him.

His mane and tail reached just to the ground, trailing softly and billowing in perfect harmony, causing him to appear to ripple as he moved.

Despite the vast throng, there was not a sound to be heard as the Great Unicorn came to a halt before me, towering above me much like Freedom had.

And, much as I had with Freedom, I extended my quivering hand.

He knelt and tilted his head to allow my fingers to reach the tip of his horn. I smiled as I remembered the scene in the castle entryway, and the joy I'd felt when Grolfshin had lifted me to reach that horn.

"Jacob, son of Prantos," the unicorn said in the beautifully deep voice I would learn that all unicorns had, "I am the Unicorn Fredriko. I speak for Portalia, and I welcome you as her guardian, her portal master, and her people's King."

SONG OF SOULS

IT'S HARD TO BELIEVE it's been a year. So much has happened.

Our search for more yellow-eyed, red-bearded lunatics came up empty. However, I doubt we will ever stop being on guard.

Grolfshin has worked hard to mend fences. People are starting to warm up to him. Especially, and most surprisingly, Bringelkoopf.

Unfortunately, it turns out that Grolfshin is quite the prankster. He and Bringelkoopf have started what looks to be a never-ending competition. The castle staff are none too pleased.

Goofing around with Bringelkoopf isn't the only way Grolfshin has revealed his new-found soft side. He was quick to adopt little Paisley, the orphaned infant of a non-Guardian fisherman who disappeared a year ago.

Grolfshin spoils his non-Guardian daughter beyond all hope. There is no trace left of the man who spent his life proclaiming the genetic superiority of Guardian bloodlines.

Strangely, Ma and Aunt Beverly were the only two in all of Portalia who were not surprised at the ease with which Paisley wrapped her new father around her chubby little fingers.

Roland took it upon himself to help me overcome my fear of water. I'm not quite there yet, but I have braved a few ocean waves. Roland is so proud of me, he says that next year we'll work on my fear of heights. I'm not so sure about that.

Fredriko is a mixture of wise old sage and rambunctious toddler. He's wicked evil with his horn when he gets into one of his giggle fits. And as an advisor, he is absolutely maddening. He is slow to tell me the things I wish to know, and quick to tell me the things I don't. Michael says that's the way of unicorns. He claims I'll never get used to it and I believe him.

Fredriko tells me that together, humans, dragons, unicorns, and eagles share one destiny. He insists he cannot explain further until I meet the dragons. Which is one of the things he is quick to remind me I need to do.

But Bringelkoopf has regaled me, far too enthusiastically, with such horrific tales of the dragons' fiery tempers that I've not been in any rush to meet them.

Which has been fine, until now. Because I must be thirteen to meet the dragons.

Except that I turn thirteen next week. And as Fredriko relishes reminding me, that means it's time to meet the dragons. And time to find out if I can build a new doorway to Earth.

Last year, I shut the last two portals to Earth. There are none left.

Not even the unicorns know who built the original ports. They know only that the Earth portals were the hardest of all to build. Rumor has it that none can ever be built again.

But I am not worried. A few weeks ago Michael shared a secret with me.

That day by the river was not the first time I met Milokah.

We had been best friends when we were little.

The day my father died Milokah and I had danced our first dance together. Afterwards, we'd made a pact that neither of us would dance again until I came back and we could dance with each other beneath the bristles in the meadow.

But I hadn't remembered. Until Michael told me.

For the pain that day had been more than I could bear.

I'd lost too much of my heart. My father. Milokah. Portalia.

That's the day that I started hiding. Hiding from all the things that could hurt me, things like memories, and love, and most of all, myself.

I started living in fear, scared to be who I was, and love who I loved.

My heart fell out of tune with my soul that day. I'd been hiding ever since.

That's why I'd sucked at everything I'd ever tried. Because I could not fit into my ears, let alone my soul, until I came out of hiding.

But for as long as I can remember, my soul had been crying out to me, whispering its yearnings to me in dreams. Dreams of my father. And of music and stars.

And dreams of a smile, one that I loved.

All those years, the smile in my dreams, the one that Jason from music camp had reminded me of, it was Milokah's smile all along.

For eight years, Milokah waited for me in the meadow. While, across the barrier of two universes, his soul called out to mine, and the two conspired to bring me back to dance with him beneath the bristles.

That's how I know I will be able to build a new portal to Earth.

For the song our souls played together, last year, when we danced beneath the bristles, was the song of souls—the song of the Portal makers.

Milokah is my love, my truth, and my destiny.

He and I still have many dances to dance with each other.

And our souls still have many songs to sing together.

OUT OF HIDING

THE BOY FROM KALATRIA didn't turn as I entered the clearing. He never did. He simply sat and stared vacantly into the crater, as he had every day since I first met him, at that very spot.

Harold's Crater.

We'd taken the boy to Kalatria village, but nobody had known who he was. So I'd taken him into my home and under my wing.

Harold continued to torment us both in our nightmares. The boy's nighttime screams will haunt me until my dying day.

I sat down beside him and together we stared into the crater.

"He's not coming back, you know," I told him.

The boy said nothing, but I would have been surprised if he had. He'd been with me for nearly a year, yet he hadn't spoken a word. I didn't even know his name.

For some reason, though, he trusted me. I think he knew that I got it—sometimes, the only safe place to hide is in your head.

Even so, I kept hoping he'd come out of hiding. I really wanted to meet him.

"How come nobody from Kalatria knows of you?" I asked him.

It was the same question I asked every day.

It was part of our ritual. I wasn't expecting an answer.

But today he surprised me.

"I'm not from Kalatria," he said, his voice soft and lilting. "I was born on Dragon's Lair. They calls me Alexario."

Then he looked at me, his eyes radiant and bright.

And his words took my breath away.

"Fredriko's right. It's time for you to meet the dragons. War is coming."

ABOUT THE AUTHOR

Casey Clubb lives near Portland, Oregon with her husband and her ever-growing collection of stuffed Tiggers.

For news and updates on Book Two—*Jacob, Portal Master*—sign up for Casey's newsletter at:

www.caseyclubb.com

MORE GREAT READS FROM BOOKTROPE

The Unintentional Time Traveler **by Everett Maroon** (Young Adult) Jack Inman's seizures aren't good for anything. Except time travel. Once he's caught in a strange place and time, falling in love is the last thing on his mind. But it may be the key to getting home.

Charis: Journey to Pandora's Jar **by Nicole Walters** (Young Adult Fantasy) Thirteen-year-old Charis Parks has five days to face her fears against the darker forces of Hades and reverse the curse of Pandora's Jar to save mankind.

A Kingdom's Possession **by Nicole Persun** (Young Adult Fantasy) A slave girl inhabited by a Goddess, loved by a Prince, hunted by a King. The beginning of an epic saga.

Dot to Dot **by Kit Bakke** (Young Adult) A teenager's touching and fantastical journey through grief. An inspiring story of adventure and travel.

Essence **by A.L. Waddington** (Young Adult) Jocelyn Timmons does not believe she is anything special. She's about to find out how wrong she is. Our minds often wander, but can our souls?

Forecast **by Elise Stephens** (Young Adult Fantasy) When teenager Calvin finds a portal that will grant him the power of prophecy, he must battle the legacies of the past and the shadows of the future to protect what is most important: his family.

Discover more books and learn about our new approach to publishing at **booktrope.com**.

CPSIA information can be obtained at www.ICGtesting.com
Printed in the USA
BVOW05s1029190714

359185BV00002B/6/P